Judy

Megan McDonald is the award-winning author
of the Judy Moody series. She says that most
of Judy's stories "grew out of anecdotes about
growing up with my four sisters". She confesses,
"I am Judy Moody. Same-same! In my family
of sisters, we're famous for exaggeration. Judy
Moody is me … exaggerated." Megan McDonald
lives with her husband in northern California.

You can find out more about Megan McDonald
and her books at **www.meganmcdonald.net**

Peter H. Reynolds says he felt an immediate
connection to Judy Moody because "having
a daughter, I have witnessed first-hand the
adventures of a very independent-minded girl".
Peter H. Reynolds lives in Massachusetts, just
down the road from his twin brother.

You can find out more about Peter H. Reynolds
and his art at **www.fablevision.com**

Books by Megan McDonald and Peter H. Reynolds

Judy Moody
Judy Moody Gets Famous!
Judy Moody Saves the World!
Judy Moody Predicts the Future
Judy Moody: The Doctor Is In!
Judy Moody Declares Independence!
Judy Moody: Around the World in $8^{1/2}$ Days
Judy Moody Goes to College
Judy Moody, Girl Detective
Judy Moody and the NOT Bummer Summer
Judy Moody and the Bad Luck Charm
Judy Moody, Mood Martian
Judy Moody and the Bucket List
Stink: The Incredible Shrinking Kid
Stink and the Incredible Super-Galactic Jawbreaker
Stink and the World's Worst Super-Stinky Sneakers
Stink and the Great Guinea Pig Express
Stink: Solar System Superhero
Stink and the Ultimate Thumb-Wrestling Smackdown
Stink and the Midnight Zombie Walk
Stink and the Freaky Frog Freakout
Stink and the Shark Sleepover
Stink-O-Pedia: Super Stinky-y Stuff from A to Zzzzz
Stink-O-Pedia 2: More Stinky-y Stuff from A to Z
Judy Moody & Stink: The Holly Joliday
Judy Moody & Stink: The Mad, Mad, Mad, Mad Treasure Hunt
Judy Moody & Stink: The Big Bad Blackout
Judy Moody & Stink : The Wishbone Wish

Books by Megan McDonald

The Sisters Club • *The Sisters Club: Rule of Three*
The Sisters Club: Cloudy with a Chance of Boys

Books by Peter H. Reynolds

The Dot • *Ish* • *So Few of Me* • *Sky Colour*

JUDY MOODY
TWICE AS MOODY

Megan McDonald

illustrated by

PeteR H. Reynolds

WALKER
BOOKS

The author extends special thanks to Hailey and Randi Reel

First published in Great Britain 2017 by Walker Books Ltd
87 Vauxhall Walk, London SE11 5HJ

2 4 6 8 10 9 7 5 3 1

Text © 2000 Megan McDonald
Illustrations © 2000 Peter H. Reynolds
Judy Moody font © 2003 Peter H. Reynolds

This book has been typeset in Stone Informal

Printed and bound in Great Britain by Clays Ltd, St Ives plc

British Library Cataloguing in Publication Data:
a catalogue record for this book is available from the British Library

ISBN 978-1-4063-7741-5

www.walker.co.uk

Judy Moody

For my sisters, Susan, Deborah, Michele, Melissa

M. M.

For my daughter, Sarah, and her cat, Twinkles

P. H. R.

A Bad Mood

Judy Moody did not want to give up summer. She did not feel like brushing her hair every day. She did not feel like memorizing spelling words. And she did not want to sit next to Frank Pearl, who ate paste, in class.

Judy Moody was in a mood.

Not a good mood. A bad mood. A mad-face mood. Even the smell of her new Grouchy pencils could not get her out of bed.

"First day of school!" sang her mother. "Shake a leg and get dressed."

Judy Moody slunk down under the covers and put a pillow over her head.

"Judy? Did you hear me?"

"ROAR!" said Judy.

She would have to get used to a new desk and a new classroom. Her new desk would not have an armadillo sticker with her name on it, like her old one last year. Her new classroom would not have a porcupine named Roger.

And with her luck, she'd get stuck sitting in the first row, where Mr Todd could see every time she tried to pass a note to her best friend, Rocky.

Mum poked her head inside Judy's room

again. "And think about brushing that hair, OK?"

One of the worst things about the first day of school was that everybody came back from summer wearing new T-shirts that said DISNEY WORLD or SEA WORLD or JAMESTOWN: HOME OF POCAHONTAS. Judy searched her top drawer and her bottom drawer and even her underwear drawer. She could not find one shirt with words.

She wore her tiger-striped pyjama pants on the bottom and a plain old no-words T-shirt on top.

"She's wearing pyjamas!" said her brother, Stink, when she came downstairs. "You can't wear pyjamas to school!"

Stink thought he knew everything now that he was starting second grade. Judy glared at him with one of her famous troll-eyes stares.

"Judy can change after breakfast," Mum said.

"I made sunny-side-up eggs for the first day of school," said Dad. "There's squishy bread for dipping."

There was nothing sunny about Judy's egg – the yellow middle was broken. Judy slid her wobbly egg into the napkin on her lap and fed it to Mouse, their cat, under the table.

"Summer is over, and I didn't even go anywhere," said Judy.

"You went to Gramma Lou's," said Mum.

"But that was right here in boring old Virginia. And I didn't get to eat hot dogs and ride a roller coaster or see a whale," said Judy.

"You rode a bumper car," said Mum.

"Baby cars. At the mall," Judy said.

"You went fishing and ate shark," said Dad.

"She ate a shark?" asked Stink.

"I ate a shark?" asked Judy.

"Yes," said Dad. "Remember the fish we bought at the market when we couldn't catch any?"

"I ate a shark!" said Judy Moody.

Judy Moody ran back to her room and peeled off her shirt. She took out a fat marker and drew a big-mouthed shark with lots of teeth. I ATE A SHARK, she wrote in capitals.

Judy ran out the door to the bus. She didn't wait for Stink. She didn't wait for kisses from Dad or hugs from Mum. She was in a hurry to show Rocky her new T-shirt with words.

She almost forgot her bad mood until she saw Rocky practising card tricks at the bus stop. He was wearing a giant-sized blue and white T-shirt with fancy letters and a picture of the Loch Ness Monster roller coaster.

"Like my new T-shirt?" he asked. "I got it at Busch Gardens."

"No," said Judy Moody, even though she secretly liked the shirt.

"I like your shark," said Rocky. When Judy didn't say anything, he asked, "Are you in a bad mood or something?"

"Or something," said Judy Moody.

Roar!

When Judy Moody arrived in third grade,
her teacher, Mr Todd, stood by the door,
welcoming everyone. "Hello there, Judy."

"Hello, Mr Toad," said Judy. She cracked
herself up.

"Class, please hang your backpacks
on the hooks and put your lunches in the
cubbies," said Mr Todd.

Judy Moody looked around the classroom. "Do you have a porcupine named

Roger?" Judy asked Mr Todd.

"No, but we have a turtle named Tucson. Do you like turtles?"

She liked turtles! But she caught herself just in time. "No. I like toads." Judy cracked up again.

"Rocky, your seat is over by the window, and Judy, yours is right up front," said Mr Todd.

"I knew it," said Judy. She surveyed her new front-row desk. It didn't have an armadillo sticker with her name on it.

Guess Who sat across the aisle from her. Frank Eats-Paste Pearl. He glanced at Judy sideways, then bent his thumb all the way back, touching his wrist. Judy rolled her tongue like a hot dog back at him.

"You like sharks too?" he asked, passing her a small white envelope with her name on it.

Ever since they had danced the maypole together in kindergarten, this boy would not leave her alone. In first grade Frank Pearl sent her five valentines. In second grade he gave her a cupcake on Halloween, on Thanksgiving and on Martin Luther King, Jr Day. Now, on the first day of third grade, he gave her a birthday party invitation. Judy checked the date inside – his birthday was not for three weeks! Even a real shark would not scare him off.

"Can I look inside your desk?" asked Judy. He moved to one side. No sign of paste.

Mr Todd stood in front of the class. GINO'S EXTRA-CHEESE PIZZA was printed in large letters on the board.

"Are we having extra-cheese pizza for lunch?" Judy asked.

"For Spelling." Mr Todd held his finger to his lips like it was a secret. "You'll see."

Then he said, "OK! Third grade! Listen up! We're going to try something different to kick off the year, as a way of getting to know one another. This year, each of you will make your own Me collage. All about YOU. You can draw or cut out pictures and paste things to your collage that tell the class what makes you YOU."

A Me collage! It sounded fun to Judy, but she didn't say so.

"We don't have to draw a map of our family, then?" asked Jessica Finch.

"I'm passing out a list of ideas for things you might include, like your family. I'm also giving everyone a folder for collecting the things you want to put on your collage.

We'll work on these as we have time over the next month. At the end of September you'll each get a chance to tell the class about YOU."

All through Language Arts and Social Studies, Judy thought about one thing – herself. Judy Moody, star of her own Me collage. Maybe third grade wasn't so bad after all.

"OK, everybody. Time for Spelling."

"Yuck. Spelling," Judy said under her breath, remembering her bad mood.

"Yuck. Spelling," Frank Pearl agreed. Judy squinched her eyebrows at him.

"Take out a piece of paper and write down five spelling words you can find hidden in the words on the board: GINO'S EXTRA-CHEESE PIZZA."

"Cool Spelling, huh?" said a note passed to Judy by Frank.

"No," she wrote back on her hand, flashing it at him.

Judy took out her brand-new package of Grouchy pencils with mad faces on them. *GROUCHY pencils – for completely impossible moods,* said the package. *L*

see a pencil that looks like it got up on the

wrong side of the bed?

Perfect. The new Grouchy pencil helped her think. She found the words TREE, TEXAS and TAXI hidden in Mr Todd's spelling on the board. But instead she wrote down (1) NO (2) NO (3) NO (4) NO (5) NO.

"Who would like to tell the class five words they came up with?" asked Mr Todd.

Judy's hand shot up.

"Judy?"

"NO, NO, NO, NO, NO!" said Judy.

"That's one word. I need four more. Come up and write them on the board."

Judy Moody did not write TREE,

TEXAS and TAXI. Instead she wrote RAT and GNAT.

"How about BRAT?" called Rocky.

"There's no *B*," said Frank Pearl.

TIGER, wrote Judy.

"One more word," said Mr Todd.

SPAT, wrote Judy.

"Can you use any of those words in a sentence, Judy?" asked Mr Todd.

"The tiger spat on the rat and the gnat."

The whole class cracked up. Frank laughed so hard he snorted.

"Are you in a bad mood today?" asked Mr Todd.

"ROAR," said Judy Moody.

"That's too bad," said Mr Todd. "I was just about to ask who wants to go down to the office and pick up the pizza. It's a welcome-back surprise."

"Pizza? Pizza! For real?" The room buzzed with excitement.

Judy Moody wanted to be the one to pick up the pizza. She wanted to be the one to open the box. She wanted to be the one who got to keep the little three-legged plastic table that kept the box top from sticking to the pizza.

"So. Who would like to pick up the pizza today?" asked Mr Todd.

"Me!" yelled Judy. "Me! Me! Me! Me! Me!" everyone shouted at once, waving their hands like windmills in the air.

Rocky raised his hand without saying a word.

"Rocky, would you like to pick up the pizza?"

"Sure!" said Rocky.

"Luck-y!" Judy said.

When Rocky came back with the pizza, the class grew quiet, everyone chewing teeny-weeny cheesy squares of Gino's pizza and listening to Mr Todd read them a chapter from a book about a pepperoni pizza-eating dog.

When he finished reading, Judy asked, "Mr Todd, can I look at your little pizza table?"

"That does look like a miniature table, Judy. I never thought of it that way."

"I collect them," said Judy Moody. She didn't really collect them – yet. So far she had collections of twenty-seven dead moths, a handful of old scabs, a dozen fancy toothpicks, hundreds of designer Band-Aids (she needed the box tops), a box of body parts (from dolls!) including three Barbie heads, and four unused erasers shaped like baseballs.

"Tell you what," said Mr Todd. "If you think you can come to third grade in a good mood tomorrow, it's yours. Do you think you can agree to that?"

"Yes, Mr Todd," said Judy. "Yes, yes, yes, yes, YES!"

pizza table ↑

Two Heads Are Better Than One

Judy was teaching Mouse to walk on two legs when the phone rang.

"Hello?"

All she heard was air.

"Hello?" Judy asked the air.

"Hello, Judy? Are you allowed to come to my party?" a voice asked. A Frank Pearl voice. It had only been two days since he gave her the invitation.

"Wrong number," said Judy, hanging up. She dangled her new pizza table from a string in front of Mouse's nose.

The phone rang again. "Hello? Is this the Moodys'?"

"Not now, Frank. I'm in the middle of an important experiment."

"OK. Bye."

The phone rang a third time.

"The experiment's not over yet," Judy yelled into the phone.

"What experiment?" asked Rocky.

"Never mind," said Judy.

"Let's go to Vic's," said Rocky. "I want to get something for my Me collage." Vic's was the minimart down the hill where they had cool prizes in the jawbreaker machine, like tattoos that washed off and magic tricks.

"Let me ask," said Judy.

"Mum, can I go to Vic's with Rocky?"

"Sure," said Mum.

"Sure!" said Judy, tossing Mouse the pizza table.

"I'm going too," said Stink.

"No, you're not," Judy told him.

"You and Rocky can take him along," said Mum, giving her one of those looks.

"But he doesn't know about crossing through China and Japan on the way," Judy said. Only best friends knew that the first speed bump on the way was crossing into China, the second, Japan.

"I'm sure you could teach him," Mum said.

"Teach me," said Stink.

"Meet me at the manhole," Judy said back into the phone. The manhole was exactly halfway between Judy's front door and Rocky's. Over the summer they had measured it with a very long ball of string.

She ran out the door. Stink ran out the door after her.

Rocky had a dollar. Judy had a dollar. Stink had six pennies.

"If we put our money together, we can buy eight jawbreakers," said Rocky.

"Two heads are better than one," Judy laughed. "Get it?" She unscrunched the dollar bill from her pocket and pointed to George Washington's head.

"I've got six heads," said Stink, showing his pennies.

"That's because you're a monster! Get it?" Judy and Rocky cracked up.

Stink did not have enough money for even one jawbreaker. "You'll break your mouth if you try to eat eight jawbreakers," said Stink. "I could eat at least two for you."

"It's for the prizes," Judy told him.

"Eight quarters give us eight chances to win a magic trick," said Rocky. "I need a new magic trick to paste on my Me collage."

"Hey, wait!" said Judy. "I just remembered – I need my dollar to buy Band-Aids."

"Band-Aids are boring," said Stink. "Besides, you have ten million. Dad says we have more Band-Aids in our bathroom than the Red Cross."

"But I want to be a doctor," said Judy. "Like Elizabeth Blackwell, First Woman Doctor! She started her own hospital. She knew how to operate and put together body parts and everything."

"Body parts. Yuck!" Stink said.

"You saved Band-Aid box tops all summer," said Rocky. "I thought you had enough to send away for that doctor doll."

"I did. I already ordered it. Back in July. I'm still waiting for it to come. But now

I need a microscope. You can look at blood or scabs or anything with it!"

Stink asked, "When do we get to China?"

"We're still on Jefferson Street, Stink," Rocky told him.

"Let's look for rocks until we get to China," said Stink.

"Let's see who can find the best one," said Rocky.

The three of them studied the ground as they walked. Judy found five pink pebbles and a Bazooka Joe comic with a fortune

5 pink pebbles   bubblegum fortune   blue lego   lucky stone

that read: MONEY IS COMING YOUR WAY.
Rocky found a blue Lego and a stone with
a hole in the middle – a lucky stone!

"I found a black diamond!" said Stink.

"That's just charcoal," said Judy.

"It's just glass," Rocky said.

"Wait!" Judy said, crossing her eyes at
Rocky. "I think it's a moon rock! Don't
you, Rocky?"

"Yes," said Rocky. "Definitely."

"How do you know?" asked Stink.

"It has craters," Judy said.

"How did it get here?" asked Stink.

"It fell from the sky," said Judy.

"Really?" asked Stink.

"Really," said Rocky. "In my *Space Junk* magazine, it tells how a moon rock fell from space and left a hole in Arizona once."

"And our teacher last year told us how a moon rock hit a dog in Egypt one time. No lie," Judy told her brother. "You're lucky. Moon rocks are billions of years old."

"*Space Junk* says moon rocks are dusty on the outside and sparkly on the inside," said Rocky.

"There's only one way to find out for sure if this is a moon rock then," said Judy. She scouted around for a large rock. Then she clobbered Stink's lump, smashing the moon rock to bits.

"You smashed it!" said Stink.

"Look, I think I see a sparkle!" said Rocky.

"Stink, you found a real moon rock, all right," Judy said.

"It's not a moon rock any more!" cried Stink.

"Look at it this way, Stink," said Judy. "Now you have something better than a moon rock."

"What could be better than a moon rock?" asked Stink.

"Lots and lots of moon dust." Judy and Rocky fell down laughing.

"I'm going home," said Stink. He scraped up handfuls of the smashed rock, filling his pockets with dirt.

Judy and Rocky laughed the rest of the way to China, ran backwards to Japan, then hopped on one foot while patting their heads until they got to Vic's.

At Vic's they put their George Washington heads together for one small box of Band-Aids, and had enough left over for one jawbreaker each. Neither of them won a magic trick for Rocky's Me collage. Not even a troll or a miniature comic book or a tattoo.

"Maybe I could put a jawbreaker on

my collage," said Rocky. "Are you going to stick some Band-Aids on yours?"

"Hey, good idea," said Judy.

"Still a nickel left," Rocky said. So they bought a gumball and saved it for Stink.

When they reached Judy's driveway, Stink ran towards them, his pockets jangling with money. Stink had brown lunch bags lined up on the front steps.

"Guess what!" called Stink. "I made three dollars! Just since I got home."

"No way," said Judy.

"Let's see," said Rocky.

Stink emptied his pockets. Rocky counted twelve quarters.

"What's in the bags?" asked Judy.

"Everybody in the state of Virginia must want it."

"Yeah, what are you selling, anyway?" asked Rocky.

"Moon dust," said Stink.

My Favourite Pet

It was Labor Day, a no-school day. Judy looked up from her Me collage on the dining-room table.

"We need a new pet," Judy announced to her family.

"A new pet? What's wrong with Mouse?" asked Mum. Mouse opened one eye.

"I have to pick MY FAVOURITE PET. How can I pick my favourite when I only have one?"

"Pick Mouse," said Mum.

"Mouse is so old, and she's afraid of everything. Mouse is a lump that purrs."

"You're NOT thinking of a dog, I hope," said Dad. Mouse jumped off the chair and stretched.

"Mouse would definitely not like that," said Judy.

"How about a goldfish?" asked Stink. Mouse rubbed up against Judy's leg.

"Mouse would like that too much," Judy said. "I was thinking of a two-toed sloth."

"Right," said Stink.

"They're neat," said Judy. She showed Stink its picture in her rainforest magazine. "See? They hang upside down all day.

They even sleep upside down."

"You're upside down," said Stink.

"What do they eat?" asked Dad.

"It says here they eat leafcutter ants and fire-bellied toads," Judy read.

"That should be easy," said Stink.

"Tell you what, Judy," said Dad. "Let's take a ride over to the pet store. I'm not saying we'll get a sloth, but it's always fun to look around. Maybe it'll even help me think of a five-letter word for fish that starts with *M* for my crossword puzzle."

"Let's all go," said Mum.

When they arrived at Fur & Fangs, Judy saw snakes and parrots, hermit crabs and guppies. She even saw a five-letter fish word beginning with *M* – a black molly.

"Do you have any two-toed sloths?" she asked the pet store lady.

"Sorry. Fresh out," said the lady.

"How about a newt or a turtle?" asked Dad.

"Did you see the hamsters?" asked Mum.

"Never mind," said Judy. "There's nothing from the rainforest here."

"Maybe they have a stink bug," Stink said.

"One's enough," said Judy, narrowing her eyes at Stink.

They picked out a squeaky toy mouse for Mouse. When they went to pay for it, Judy noticed a green plant with teeth sitting on the counter. "What's that?" she asked the pet store lady.

"A Venus flytrap," the lady said. "It's not an animal, but it doesn't cost much, and it's easy to take care of. See these things that look like mouths with teeth? Each one closes like a trapdoor. It eats bugs around the house. Like flies and ants, that sort of thing. You can feed it a little raw hamburger too."

"Rare," said Judy Moody.

"Cool," said Stink.

"Good idea," said Mum.

"Sold," said Dad.

Judy set her new pet on her desk, where the angle of sunlight hit it just right. Mouse watched from the bottom bunk, with one eye open.

"I can't wait to take my new pet to school tomorrow for Share and Tell," Judy told Stink. "It's just like a rare plant from the rainforest."

"It is?" Stink asked.

"Sure," said Judy. "Just think. There could be a medicine hiding right here in these funny green teeth. When I'm a doctor, I'm going to study plants like this and discover cures for ucky diseases."

"What are you going to name it?" asked Stink.

"I don't know yet," said Judy.

"You could call it Bughead, since it likes bugs."

"Nah," said Judy.

Judy watered her new pet. She sprinkled Gro-Fast on the soil. When Stink left, she sang songs to it. "I know an old lady who swallowed a fly…" She sang till the old lady swallowed a horse.

She still couldn't think of a good name. Rumpelstiltskin? Too long. Thing? Maybe.

"Stink!" she called. "Go get me a fly."

"How am I going to catch a fly?" asked Stink.

"One fly. I'll give you a dime."

Stink ran down to the window behind the couch and brought back a fly.

"Gross! That fly is dead."

"It was going to be dead in a minute anyway."

Judy scooped up the dead fly with the tip of her ruler and dropped it into one of the mouths. In a flash the trap closed round the fly. Just like the pet store lady said.

"Rare!" said Judy.

"Snap! Trap!" Stink said, adding sound effects.

"Go get me an ant. A live one this time."

Here's one...

...a real beauty!

Here anty, anty!

No way!

Snap! Trap!

Urp!

Stink wanted to see the Venus flytrap eat again, so he got his sister an ant. "Snap! Trap!" said Judy and Stink when another trap closed.

"Double rare," Judy said. "Stink, go catch me a spider or something."

"I'm tired of catching bugs," said Stink.

"Then go ask Mum or Dad if we have any raw hamburger."

Stink frowned.

"Please, pretty please with bubblegum ice cream on top?" Judy begged. Stink didn't budge. "I'll let you feed it this time."

Stink ran to the kitchen and came back with a hunk of raw hamburger. He plopped a big glob of hamburger into an open trap.

"That's way too much!" Judy yelled, but

it was too late. The mouth snap-trapped round it, hamburger oozing out of its teeth. In a blink the whole arm drooped, collapsing in the dirt.

"You killed it! You're in trouble, Stink. MUM! DAD!" Judy called.

Judy showed her parents what happened. "Stink killed my Venus flytrap!"

"I didn't mean to," said Stink. "The trap closed really fast!"

"It's not dead. It's digesting," said Dad.

"The jaws will probably open by tomorrow morning," said Mum.

"Maybe it's just sleeping or something," said Stink.

"Or something," said Judy.

My Smelly Pet

Tomorrow morning came. The jaws were still closed. Judy tried teasing it with a brand-new ant. "Here you go," she said in her best squeaky baby voice. "You like ants, don't you?" The jaws did not open one tiny centimetre. The plant did not move one trigger hair.

Judy gave up. She carefully lodged the plant in the bottom of her backpack.

She'd take it to school, stinky, smelly glob of hamburger and all.

On the bus Judy showed Rocky her new pet. "I couldn't wait to show everybody how it eats. Now it won't even move. And it smells."

"Open sesame!" said Rocky, trying some magic words. Nothing happened.

"Maybe," said Rocky, "the bus will bounce it open."

"Maybe," said Judy. But even the bouncing of the bus did not make her new pet open up.

"If this thing dies, I'm stuck with Mouse for MY FAVOURITE PET," Judy said.

Mr Todd said first thing, "OK, class, take out your Me collage folders. I'll pass around old magazines, and you can spend the next half-hour cutting out pictures for your collages. You still have over three weeks, but I'd like to see how everybody's doing."

Her Me collage folder! Judy had been so busy with her new pet, she had forgotten to bring her folder to school.

Judy Moody sneaked a peek at Frank Pearl's folder. He had cut out pictures of macaroni (favourite food?), ants (favourite pet?) and shoes. Shoes? Frank Pearl's best friend was a pair of shoes?

Judy looked down at the open backpack under her desk. The jaws were still closed. Now her whole backpack was smelly. Judy took the straw from her juice box and poked at the Venus flytrap. No luck. It would never open in time for Share and Tell!

"Well?" Frank asked.

"Well, what?"

"Are you going to come?"

"Where?"

"My birthday party. A week from Saturday. All the boys from our class are coming. And Adrian and Sandy from next door."

Judy Moody did not care if the president himself was coming. She sniffed her backpack. It stunk like a skunk!

"What's in your backpack?" Frank asked.

"None of your beeswax," Judy said.

"It smells like dead tuna fish!" Frank Pearl said. Judy hoped her Venus flytrap would come back to life and bite Frank Pearl before he ever had another birthday.

Mr Todd came over. "Judy, you haven't cut out any pictures. Do you have your folder?"

"I did – I mean – it was – then – well – no," said Judy. "I got a new pet last night."

"Don't tell me," said Mr Todd. "Your new pet ate your Me collage folder."

"Not exactly. But it did eat one dead fly and one live ant. And then a big glob of—"

"Next time try to remember to bring your folder to school, Judy. And please, everyone, keep homework away from animals!"

"My new pet's not an animal, Mr Todd," Judy said. "And it doesn't eat homework. Just bugs and raw hamburger." She pulled the Venus flytrap from her backpack. Judy could not believe her eyes! Its arm was no longer droopy. The stuck trap

was now wide open, and her plant was
looking hungry.

"It's MY FAVOURITE PET," said Judy.
"Meet Jaws!"

Doctor Judy Moody

Finally! Judy thought the only thing finer in the world than getting Jaws had to be getting a big brown box in the mail with the name DOCTOR JUDY MOODY on it. She was in an operating mood.

"Can I open it?" asked Stink, coming out of his closet fort.

"What does it say right there?" asked Judy, pointing to the label.

"DOCTOR JUDY MOODY," read Stink.

"Exactly," said Judy Moody. "I collected all the box tops."

"I got you some from the school nurse!" said Stink.

"OK. You can go get the scissors."

Stink handed over the scissors. Judy poked through the tape and broke open the brown flaps. Mouse pawed at the sticky tape. Stink's head kept getting in the way.

"Stink! I'm in the middle of an operation!" Judy pulled aside the tissue paper and lifted out the doctor doll.

At last! Judy held the doll in her lap and stroked her silky smooth hair. She made neat little bows in the ties of the doll's blue and white hospital gown. The doll was wearing a hospital bracelet.

"Her name is Hedda-Get-Betta," Judy read.

"Does she do anything?" asked Stink.

"It says here if you turn the knob on top of her head, she gets sick. Then you turn the knob again, and she gets betta. Get it?"

Judy turned the knob on the doll's head until a new face appeared. "She has measles!" said Stink.

"She talks when you hug her too." Judy hugged the doll.

"I have measles," said Hedda-Get-Betta.

Judy turned the knob until another face appeared. Then she hugged the doll again.

"I have chickenpox," said Hedda-Get-Betta.

"Cool," said Stink. "A sick doll. With three heads."

Judy turned the knob once more and hugged the doll. "All better," said Hedda.

"Can I make her get sick, then better?" asked Stink.

"No," said Judy. "I'm the doctor."

Judy opened her doctor kit. "At last I have someone to practise on," she said.

"You practise on me all the time," said Stink.

"Someone who doesn't complain."

"You'd complain too if you had to hold

up a lamp and get bandages all over you. Why can't I ever be Elizabeth Blackwell, First Woman Doctor?"

"For one thing, you're a boy."

"Can I put her arm in a sling?" asked Stink.

"No," said Judy. She held the ear scope up to Hedda's ear and turned on the light.

"Can I mix up some of this blood from your doctor kit?"

"Shh, I'm listening." She held the stethoscope on Hedda. Then she held it on Stink's chest. "Hmm."

"What?" said Stink. "What do you hear?"

"A heartbeat. This can mean only one thing."

"What?"

"You're alive!"

"Can I listen for a heartbeat?"

"OK, OK. But first get me a glass of water to mix the blood in."

"You get it," said Stink.

"Don't touch anything until I get back," said Judy. "Don't even breathe."

As soon as Judy rounded the corner, Stink turned the knob on the doll's head. Measles. He turned the knob again. Chickenpox. Measles. Chickenpox. Measles. Chickenpox. Stink turned Hedda-Get-Betta's head back and forth, over and over, faster and faster.

"Uh-oh," said Stink.

"What?" Judy asked, returning with a sloshing glass of water.

"Her head is stuck," he said. Judy grabbed Hedda-Get-Betta away from Stink.

"I have chickenpox," Hedda said. Judy tried to turn the knob. The knob was stuck all right. It would not turn, no matter how hard Judy twisted and yanked and pulled. "I have chickenpox. I have chickenpox," Hedda said again and again.

"Her head is stuck on chickenpox!" Judy moaned.

"It's not my fault," said Stink.

"Is too! Now she'll never get better!" Judy took Hedda's pulse. She listened to Hedda's heart. She checked Hedda's forehead for a fever. "My first patient, and she's going to have chickenpox for the rest of her life!"

Judy took the doll to her mother. But Mum could not turn the knob, even with her best opening-pickle-jars twist. Judy took the doll to her father. But Dad could not get the doll's head to turn, even with his best opening-spaghetti-sauce turn.

"What are you going to do?" asked Dad.

"There's only one thing I can think of."

"Give her a shot?" asked Mum.

"No," said Judy. "Band-Aids!"

"Cool!" said Stink.

Stink and Judy put fancy Band-Aids on Hedda-Get-Betta's face, one for every chicken pock. Then they put Band-Aids all over her body. There were Endangered Species Band-Aids, Dinosaurs, Tattoos, Mermaids and Race Cars. Even Glow-in-the-Dark Bloodshot-Eyeball Band-Aids.

"So she won't scratch," said Doctor Judy.

"I'm glad that emergency's over," Dad said.

Judy tried to turn the doll's head one last time. She did not yank or twist or pull. She very slowly, very carefully turned the knob. Hedda's head turned, and her smiling, no-chickenpox face reappeared.

"I cured her!" Judy yelled. She hugged her doll. "All better," said Hedda-Get-Betta.

"Good as new," said Mum and Dad.

"I'm just glad she didn't have spotted fever," said Judy. "I never in a million years would have had enough Band-Aids for that!"

The TP Club

"I think it's going to rain for forty days and forty nights," said Stink.

Judy was hanging blankets from her top bunk to make a rainforest canopy over her bottom bunk. When that was done, she set Jaws on the top bunk for a jungly effect. Who needed a two-toed sloth? She climbed in and spread out her Me collage. Mouse climbed in after her. "Don't get hair on my collage," Judy warned her.

Stink stuck his head through the blankets.

"Who's that with hair sticking all out?" he asked, pointing to her collage.

"That's me in a bad mood on the first day of school."

"Where's me? Don't they need to know about brothers?"

"You mean *bothers*?" asked Judy.

She pointed to some dirt glued in the lower left-hand corner.

"I'm dirt?" asked Stink.

Judy cracked up. "That's for selling moon dust," said Judy.

"What's that blob? Blood?"

"Red. MY FAVOURITE COLOUR."

"Are those Spider Web Band-Aids?" Stink asked. "Where'd you get glitter glue? Can I come in there and glitter glue my bat wings?"

Her little brother, the bat freak, was becoming a regular Frank Pearl.

"There's no room, Stink. This is serious. I only have about two more weeks to finish."

Judy cut out a picture of Hedda from the ad in her *Luna Girls* magazine and pasted it in the doctor corner, right next to her drawing of Elizabeth Blackwell copied from an encyclopedia.

She checked Mr Todd's list of collage ideas.

CLUBS. I don't belong to any clubs,

thought Judy. She'd have to skip that one.

HOBBIES. Collecting things was her favourite hobby. But she couldn't paste a scab or a Barbie head to the collage. She taped on the pizza table from her newest collection – the one Mr Todd had given her.

THE WORST THING THAT EVER HAPPENED. She couldn't think of anything. Maybe the worst thing that ever happened to her hadn't happened yet.

THE FUNNIEST THING THAT EVER HAPPENED. When I knocked real spooky on the wall of Stink's room one night and scared him, she thought. But how could she put that on a collage?

Judy puzzled over her Me collage until the rain finally stopped. She called Rocky.

"Meet me at the manhole in five," she told him.

Rocky wore his boa constrictor shirt. Judy wore her boa constrictor shirt. "Same-same!" said Judy and Rocky, slapping hands together twice in a high five, the way they always had when they did something exactly alike.

Judy and Rocky stood on the manhole. "What do you think is under the street?" asked Rocky.

"Oodles and oodles of worms," said Judy.

"Let's collect some in the street and throw them down there," said Rocky.

"Too oogey," said Judy.

"We could look for rainbows in puddles," Rocky suggested.

"Too hard!" said Judy.

"Listen," said Rocky. "I hear toads. We could catch toads!"

Rocky ran back home to get a bucket. When he came back, they cornered a toad and popped the bucket on top of it.

"Gotcha!" Judy held it in her hand. "It feels soft and bumpy. It's kind of cool, but not slimy."

All of a sudden Judy felt something warm and wet in her hand. "Yuck!" she cried. "That toad peed on me." She tossed the toad back into the bucket.

"It's probably just wet from the rain," Rocky said.

"Oh, yeah? Then you pick it up."

Rocky picked up the toad. He held it in

his hand. It felt soft and bumpy and cool-but-not-slimy all at once.

Just then Rocky felt something warm and wet in his hand. "Yuck," Rocky cried. "Now that toad peed on me." He tossed the toad back into the bucket.

"See what I mean?" said Judy. "I can't believe it happened to both of us the same!"

"Same-same!" said Rocky, and they double-high-fived. "Now it's like we're members of the same club. A secret club that only the two of us know about."

"And now we have a club to put on our Me collages," said Judy.

"What should we call it?" asked Rocky.

"The Toad Pee Club!"

"Rare!" said Rocky. "We could put TP

Club on our collages. People will think it stands for the Toilet Paper Club."

"Perfect," Judy said.

"Hey, what are you two doing?" asked Stink, running down the sidewalk in too-big boots.

"Nothing," said Judy, wiping her hands down the sides of her pants.

"Yes, you are," said Stink. "I can tell by your caterpillar eyebrows."

"What caterpillar eyebrows?"

"Your eyebrows make a fuzzy caterpillar when you don't want to tell me something."

Judy Moody never knew she had caterpillar eyebrows before.

"Yeah, a stinging caterpillar," said Judy.

"We're starting a club," said Rocky.

"A secret club," Judy said quickly.

"I like secrets," said Stink. "I want to be in the club."

"You can't just be in the club," said Judy. "Something has to happen to you."

"I want the thing to happen to me too."

"No, you don't," said Judy.

"It's yucky," Rocky said.

"What?" asked Stink.

"Never mind," said Judy.

"You have to pick up that toad," Rocky told Stink.

"This is a trick, isn't it?" asked Stink. "To get me to pick up a slimy, bumpy old toad."

"That's right," said Judy.

Stink picked up the toad anyway. "Hey, it feels … interesting. Like a pickle. I never picked up a toad before," said Stink. "Now can I be in the club?"

"No," said Judy.

"I can't believe it's not slimy," said Stink.

"Just wait," said Rocky.

"I'm not going to get warts or anything, am I?"

"Do you feel anything?" asked Rocky.

"No," said Stink.

"Oh, well," said Judy. "Put the toad back. There. See? You can't be in the club."

Stink started to cry. "But I picked up the toad, and I want to be in the club."

"Don't cry," said Judy. "Trust me, Stink, you don't want to be in this club."

Just then Stink's eyes opened very wide. There was something warm and wet on his hand. Judy Moody and Rocky fell down laughing.

"Am I in the club yet?" asked Stink.

"Yes! Yes! Yes!" said Judy and Rocky. "The Toad Pee Club!"

"Yippee!" cried Stink. "I'm in the Toad Pee Club!"

The Worst Thing Ever

D-day. Doomsday. Dumbday. Saturday. The day of Frank Eats-Paste Pearl's birthday party. I'd rather eat ten jars of paste myself than go to that party, Judy thought.

For three whole weeks she had kept the hand-delivered-by-Frank-Pearl birthday invitation hidden inside the bottom of her Tip-It game, where Mum and Dad (who hated Tip-It) would NEVER find it.

Then today, the very day of the party, it happened. Dad found out.

She, Judy Moody, just had to ask Dad to take her to Fur & Fangs for some toad food. She just happened to be looking at a tadpole kit with real live frog eggs – *Watch tadpoles turn into frogs! See tails shrink, feet grow, legs form!* – hoping to talk Dad into buying it for her when another kit just like it bumped into her. Holding the kit was Frank's mum.

"Judy!" Frank's mum said. "Isn't that funny? It looks like we had the same idea for Frank's present! I thought he'd love watching a tadpole turn into a frog. I was about to buy him the same kit!"

"Um, I wasn't … I mean, you were?"

"Frank's really looking forward to seeing you at his party."

"Party?" Dad's ears perked up. "Whose party?"

"Frank's!" said his mum. "I'm Mrs Pearl, Frank's mum."

"Nice to meet you," said Dad.

"Very nice to meet *you*," said Mrs Pearl. "And Judy, I'll see you this afternoon. Bye for now."

Mrs Pearl put the tadpole kit she was holding back on the shelf.

"Frank LOVES reptiles," she said.

Amphibians, thought Judy.

"Judy, why didn't you just say you needed to come here to get your friend a birthday present? Did I know you had a party to go to today?" Dad asked.

"No."

In the car Judy tried to convince her Dad that there would be kids at the party making rude body noises and calling each other animal-breath names.

"You'll have fun."

"You know, Frank Pearl eats paste," said Judy.

"Look. You've already got the tadpole kit," Dad said.

"I was kind of sort of hoping I could keep it."

"But Mrs Pearl put hers back when she saw yours. At least take it over, Judy."

"Do I have to wrap it?" asked Judy.

From the look on his face, she knew the answer.

Judy Moody wrapped the too-good-for-a-paste-eater present in boring newspaper (not the comics). Even though the party started at two o'clock, she told Mum and Dad that it didn't start until four o'clock, so she would only have to go for the last disgusting minutes.

The whole family rode in the car to Frank Pearl's house. Even Toady went along, carried by Stink in a yogurt container. Judy held Frank's lumpy present and fell into a bad-mood backseat slump. Why did Rocky have to go to his grandma's TODAY of all days?

"She's crying!" Stink reported to the front seat.

"Am not!" she said back with her best troll eyes ever.

"Wait here," Judy told her family when they got to Frank's house.

"Go ahead. Have fun," Dad said. "We'll be back for you in half an hour. Forty minutes tops."

"We're only going to the supermarket," said Mum. But they might as well have been going to New Zealand.

Mrs Pearl answered the door. "Judy! We thought you'd changed your mind. C'mon out back. Fra-ank. Judy's here, honey," Mrs Pearl called out to the back-yard.

Judy looked around the yard. All she could see were boys. Boys hurling icing insects at each other and boys mixing chocolate cake with ketchup and boys conducting an experiment with Kool-Aid and a grasshopper.

"Where are the other kids?" asked Judy.

"Everybody's here, honey. Frank's little sister, Maggie, went off to a friend's. I think you know all the boys from school. And there's Adrian and Sandy from next door."

Sandy was a boy. So was Adrian. That Frank Pearl had tricked her – the girls next door were boys! She, Judy Moody, was definitely the one and only girl. Alone. At Frank Pearl's all-boy-except-her birthday party!

Judy wanted to climb right up Frank Pearl's tyre-swing rope and howl like a rainforest monkey. Instead she asked, "Do you have a bathroom?"

Judy decided to stay in the Pearls' bathroom for ever. Or at least until her parents came back from New Zealand. Frank Pearl's all-boy party had to be THE WORST THING THAT EVER HAPPENED to her.

Judy looked for something to do. Uncapping an eyebrow pencil, she drew some sharp new teeth on her faded first-day-of-school shark T-shirt. Rare.

Knock knock.

"Ju-dy? Are you in there?"

Judy turned on the water in a hurry so Mrs Pearl would think she was washing her hands.

"Just a minute!" she called. Water sprayed her all over, soaking her shirt. The sharp new shark teeth blurred and ran.

Judy opened the door. Mrs Pearl said, "Frank was about to open your present, but we couldn't find you."

Back outside, Brad pointed at Judy's wet shirt. "You guys! It's a shark! With black blood dripping from its mouth!"

"Cool!"

"Wow!"

"How'd you do that?"

"Talent," said Judy. "And water."

"Water fight!" Brad took a glass of water and threw it on Adam. Mitchell threw one at Dylan. Frank poured one right over his own head and grinned.

Mrs Pearl whistled, which put a stop to the water battle. "Dylan! Brad! Your parents are here. Don't forget your party favours." Mrs Pearl gave a baby Slinky to each kid as he went out the door. By the time she got to Judy, there were no more baby Slinkies left.

"I must have counted wrong," said Mrs Pearl.

"Or Brad took two," said Frank.

"Here, Judy. I was going to buy these for party favours, but I

108

couldn't find enough." Mrs Pearl handed her a miniature rock and gem collection in a plastic see-through box! Tiny amethyst and jade stones. Even a crackly amber one.

"Thank you, Mrs Pearl!" Judy said, and she meant it. "I love collecting stones and things. Once my brother thought he found a real moon rock!"

"Frank's a collector too," said Mrs Pearl. "All the boys are gone, Frank. Why don't you take Judy up to your room and show her while she waits for her parents?"

"C'mon. Last one up's a rotten banana!" said Frank.

He probably collects paste jars, Judy thought. He probably eats it for a midnight snack.

Frank Pearl's shelves were lined with coffee cans and baby food jars. Each one was filled with marbles, rubber bugs, erasers, something. Judy couldn't help asking, "Do you have any baseball erasers?"

"I have ten!" said Frank. "I got them FREE when a real Oriole came to the library."

"Really? Me too!" Judy smiled. She almost said "Same-same" but caught herself just in time.

"I'm taping one to my Me collage, beside my favourite bug, a click beetle, for HOBBIES – you know, collecting things."

"That's my hobby too," Judy told him.

He also had two pencil sharpeners – a Liberty Bell and a brain – and a teeny-tiny flip-book from Vic's. Frank Pearl showed her his buffalo nickel, which he kept in a double-locked piggy bank. "It's not really a collection yet because there's only one."

"That's OK," said Judy.

Frank also had a killer comic book collection, with really old ones like *The Green Hornet*, *Richie Rich*, and *Captain Marvel*. To top it off, he even had a miniature soap collection, with fancy hotel names on the wrappers.

Judy forgot all about wanting to leave. "What's that?" she asked.

"A pitcher plant. It catches insects. They think it's a flower, so they land on it.

Then they fall down this tube, and the plant eats them."

"Rare!" said Judy. "I have a Venus flytrap named Jaws."

"I know," said Frank. "That was funny when you brought it to school, how it ate that hamburger and stunk up your backpack and everything."

"Fra-ank! Ju-dy! The Moodys are here."

"I guess I gotta go," Judy told Frank.

"Well, thanks for the tadpole kit," Frank said, twisting a leg of the rubber click beetle from his collection.

"Hey, do you really eat paste?" asked Judy.

"I tasted it one time. For a dare."

"Rare!" Judy said.

Definitely the Worst Thing Ever

Judy's day was off to a grouchy start. This was the day that Stink, her once smelly, sold-dirt-for-moon-dust brother was going with his class to Washington, DC, to see the president's house!

She found out Mum and Dad were going too, as chaperones.

Yours Truly had to stay home and finish her Me collage. She, Judy Moody, still had several bald spots to fill.

"I think my brain has a leak," Judy told her family. "I can't think of one more interesting thing to put on my collage."

Judy sank down on the family-room couch like a balloon that had lost three days' air. "Interesting things could happen to me better in Washington, DC," said Judy.

"You know it's just for the second grade classes, honey," said Mum.

"ROAR!" was all she said.

"We might be home late," Dad told her. "You can go to Rocky's after school. You two can finish up your projects together."

"You'll have fun," said Mum. "And aren't you going to an assembly today for Brush Your Teeth Week?"

How could she forget? One more reason to be grouchy. Stink got to rub elbows with the president while she, Judy Moody, would be shaking the hands of Mr Tooth and Mrs Floss.

Stink waddled into the family room wrapped in a red and white striped table-cloth, looking like he just got hit by a flying picnic.

"What's that?" asked Judy.

"It's a costume for my YOU ARE THE FLAG project. I'm the flag."

"Stink, you're not supposed to *be* the flag. You're supposed to tell what the flag means to you."

"To me it means I *am* the flag."

"What's on your head?"

"A hat. See, each star is a state, like on the flag. There's one for all forty-eight states."

"Guess what. There are fifty states, Stink."

"Nuh-uh. I counted. I crossed them off on my map."

"Count again," Judy said. "You probably forgot Hawaii and Alaska."

"Do you think the president will notice?" asked Stink.

"Stink, the president just about made the states. He'll notice."

"OK, OK. I'll stick two more on."

"Every other second grader writes a flag poem or draws a picture for YOU ARE THE FLAG. *My* brother's a human flag."

"What's wrong with that?"

"You look like a star-spangled mummy and walk like a banana. That's what."

"I get to see a room where everything is made of real gold. Even the curtains and bedspreads. Heather Strong says the lamps are made of diamonds."

"Heather Strong lies," said Judy.

It was no use. She would have to change her Me collage. Frank's birthday party was no longer THE WORST THING EVER. Frank Pearl ate paste for a dare! And he gave her a baby food jar with six ants and a fly for Jaws.

Not meeting the president of her own United fifty States was absolutely and positively THE WORST THING THAT EVER

HAPPENED. Her whole family, including her brother, the human flag, was going to Washington, DC, while she, Judy Moody, would be listening to a talking tooth.

The Funniest Thing Ever

It was pouring outside. Judy's dad would not let her leave for school without an umbrella, and the only one she could find was her first grade yellow ducky one. She wouldn't open a baby umbrella, so she got soaked clear through. The sun is probably shining over the president's house this second, thought Judy. She felt like a bike left out in the rain.

"Frank wants to come over after school too," Rocky told her on the bus. "And I have a brand-new ten-dollar bill from Nay-Nay. We can go to Vic's after school and buy something really rare."

"Do they have any real gold at Vic's?" was all she said.

In Spelling Judy wrote WEASELS when Mr Todd had really said MEASLES. In Science when Jessica Finch threw Judy the ball of yarn for their giant spider web, she dropped it. It rolled out the door just when Ms Tuxedo, the principal, walked past in high heels. And at the Brush Your Teeth Week assembly, Mr Tooth picked Judy to be a cavity. On stage. In front of the whole school.

She could not get her mind off Stink at the president's house, where *she* wasn't. Seeing all that real gold. Would he get to shake the president's hand? Meet the president's daughter? Sit in a gold chair?

"Are flags allowed to talk?" she asked Frank.

"Only if they're talking flags!"

That did it. There would be no living with Stink once he had been to the president's.

On the bus ride home, Rocky squirted Frank with his magic nickel. Frank snorted, wiping the drips on his sleeve. Judy pretended it was funny. Really she was thinking, Stink could be petting the president's puppy right now, this very instant. When Rocky said, "I can't wait to go to Vic's," Judy grunted.

The three of them half ran through leftover puddles all the way to Vic's. Rocky didn't even stop to cross through China and Japan the right way. "What's the big hurry?" she asked.

"I need something," said Rocky, "but there's only one left, and I want to make sure I get it!" he said. When they got to Vic's, Rocky went straight to the counter.

"Over here," Rocky told them. "There's still one left!"

Judy stood on tiptoe to look in a box on top of the counter. Lying in the bottom was ... a hand. A person's hand! Judy almost screamed. Frank almost screamed too. Then they realized it was made out of rubber.

"What do you think?" asked Rocky.

"Rare," said Judy.

"Ace," said Frank. "It looks so real. Fingernails and everything!"

Rocky bought the hand and three fireballs.

"What are you going to do with your hand?" Frank asked.

"I don't know," said Rocky. "I just like it."

When they got to Rocky's house, Judy tried to work on her Me collage. But she was not in a FUNNIEST THING EVER mood. All the funny stuff that had ever happened to her seemed to have got up and left. Marched right out of her brain like a line of ants from a picnic.

Rocky showed Judy and Frank his finished collage.

"Here's Thomas Jefferson in the window of my house for WHERE I LIVE. I cut him out of play money."

"That's good!" said Frank. "For Jefferson Street."

"The piece of cloth is part of my sling from when I broke my arm, THE WORST

THING EVER. And here's a toilet paper roll for the TP Club, a secret club I'm in," Rocky said, glancing at Judy.

"What kind of club has toilet paper?" asked Frank.

"If I tell you, it won't be a secret."

"Who's this?" Frank asked Rocky, pointing to a lizard.

"Houdini, MY FAVOURITE PET."

"And who's that guy, walking through a brick wall?" Frank asked.

"That's my favourite part. My mum made a copy of a picture of the real Harry Houdini from a library book."

Judy touched a clump of garlic. "Are you trying to scare away vampires or something?"

"That's from one time when I ate a whole thing of garlic by mistake. THE FUNNIEST THING EVER was that I stunk like a skunk for a week!"

"Like Jaws when it ate that hamburger!" said Frank.

"Like Stink when he takes his smelly shoes off," said Judy.

"Is this you?" Frank asked.

"That's me in my magician hat, making a fishbowl disappear."

"Too bad you can't make Stink disappear," said Judy.

"Too bad I'm done," said Rocky. "It would have been really funny to put the rubber hand on my collage."

That's when it happened. An idea. The funniest of all funnies. It orbited Judy's head and landed like a spaceship, the way good ideas do.

"Rocky! You're a genius! Let's go to my

house," Judy said. "And bring the hand."

"You're *not* a genius," said Rocky. "Nobody's home at your house. We could get into all kinds of trouble."

"Exactly!" said Judy. "C'mon. There's a key hidden in the gutter pipe."

"Did you forget something?" asked Frank.

"Yes," Judy said. "I forgot to play a trick on Stink!"

Once inside, Judy raced around her house, looking for the perfect spot to leave the hand, a place where Stink would be sure to find it right away. The couch? Toady's aquarium? The refrigerator? Under his pillow?

The bathroom!

Where?

Here?

How about here?

Hmm...

Or here?

Maybe here?

I've got it!

Perfect!

In the downstairs bathroom Judy lifted up the toilet seat, just a crack, and perched the hand there, its fingernails hanging over the edge. "It looks real," said Rocky.

"This will scare the president right out of him," said Judy. "For sure."

Back at Rocky's, Judy, Frank and Rocky knelt on Rocky's bed, looking out the window. Every time a car zoomed by on Jefferson Street, they yelled, "It's them!" Finally Judy saw a blue van for real. "Run!" she yelled. "They're pulling into the driveway!"

Stink was so excited telling Judy, Rocky and Frank all about the president's house that Hawaii and Alaska fell off his hat.

Why doesn't he go to the bathroom? thought Judy.

"There's a movie theatre – I swear! Inside the president's house. And a room with a secret door. No lie. Even a clock that tells you when it's time to take a bath," said Stink.

"Rare!" said Judy. "You need one of those."

Go into the bathroom, Stink, she wished silently. As if he had heard, Stink stopped his story. Balancing his hat on his head, he walked into the bathroom and shut the door behind him. The lock clicked.

Mum and Dad asked Judy about the Mr Tooth assembly, but her ears were tuned to the bathroom.

"AAAAAHHHHH!" screamed Stink. He burst out of the bathroom, hat crashing to the floor, stars flying.

"Hey! Dad! Mum! There's somebody in the toilet!"

Judy Moody, Rocky and Frank Pearl fell on the floor laughing.

The Me Collage

Stink watched Judy finish her collage after school the next day. "Almost done," said Judy. "It's due tomorrow."

Stink pointed. "You still have a bald spot right there next to the picture of Jaws."

Judy carefully taped a doll hand from her collection over the empty space. "Not any more," she said.

"That hand? Is it for the trick you played on me?" asked Stink.

"Yes. It's THE FUNNIEST THING EVER," said Judy with a grin.

"You mean you're going to tell your whole class I thought there was somebody in our toilet?"

"Stink, I'm making you famous."

"Couldn't you change my name or something?" asked Stink.

"Or something," said Judy.

When Judy got up the next morning, it was pouring with rain again. Something told her to get ready for a bad-mood Friday.

"Let's put your Me collage in a garbage bag so it won't get wet," Dad suggested when she brought it downstairs.

"Dad, I'm not carrying my Me collage in a garbage bag."

"Why not?"

"Did Van Gogh put his *Starry Night* in a garbage bag?"

"She's got a point there," said Mum.

"Garbage bags probably hadn't been invented yet," said Dad. "If Van Gogh had garbage bags, believe me, he would have been smart enough to use them."

"Honey, why don't you take the bus, and Dad'll bring your collage to school after he takes Stink to the dentist?" Mum said. "Stink's taking Toady to school today, so Dad has to drop him off anyway."

"I want to take my collage to school myself. That way I can be sure nothing will happen to it."

"What could happen to it?" asked Mum.

"There could be a tornado," said Stink, "and the wind could make you drop it, and it could get run over by a bus."

"Hardee-har-har," said Judy.

"You do have a lot of other stuff to carry," said her dad. Judy had her lunch, her dad's lab coat so she could dress like a doctor for her talk, Hedda-Get-Betta, her doctor kit and plenty of Band-Aids.

"OK," she said, "but don't squish anything and don't get it wet and it has to be there by eleven o'clock and don't let Stink do *anything.*" She gave her brother her best troll-eyes stare.

"We'll be careful," said Dad.

Judy rode the bus with Rocky, who

practised his squirting nickel magic trick on her for the one hundredth time.

"OK! It works!" Judy told him, wiping drips from her face. Rocky cracked up.

All morning Judy imagined things happening to her collage. What if it fell into a puddle when her father opened the car door? What if Toady got out of Stink's pocket and peed on the collage? What if a tornado came, like Stink said…

Eleven o'clock came, and her collage still was not there. No sign of Stink. Or Dad.

Judy could hardly listen to the other kids showing their Me collages. She kept her eyes glued to the door of 3T.

"Judy, would you like to go next?" asked Mr Todd, startling her.

"I'd like to go last," said Judy.

"Frank?"

"I'd like to go last too," said Frank. "After Judy."

Judy looked at Frank's desk. "Where's your Me collage?" she asked him.

"I didn't bring it. I mean, I'm not finished. I still don't have a CLUB," Frank whispered. "Where's yours?"

"My brother's supposed to bring it," said Judy. She glanced at the door again. There he was! Stink motioned for her to come out in the hall.

Stink looked sick. "What's wrong?" Judy asked.

"If I tell you," said Stink, "you'll be in the worst mood ever."

"Where is it?" asked Judy. "Did you drop my collage in a puddle? Did Toady pee on it?"

"No," said Stink. "Not that."

"Where is it?" she asked again.

"Dad's in the boys' room. Drying it off."

Judy ran down to the boys' room, pushed the door open and went right in. Crumpled paper towels were everywhere. "Dad!"

"Judy!"

"Is it ruined? Let me see!"

Dad held up her collage. Right smack dab in the centre was a big purple stain the size of a pancake. Not a silver dollar one either. A giant, jaggedy triangle – a grape-coloured lake floating in the middle of her collage!

"What happened?" Judy yelled.

"I was drinking Jungle Juice from a box," said Stink, standing behind her in the doorway, "and trying this thing with my straw... I'm sorry."

"Stink! You wrecked it. Dad! How could you let him drink Jungle Juice in the car?"

"Look, it's not that bad," he said. "It almost looks like it's supposed to be there. I'll speak with Mr Todd. Maybe he'll let you have the weekend and we can fix it. Cover it up somehow."

"Maybe we can erase it," said Stink. "With a giant eraser."

"Let me see." Judy held up the collage, looking it over. Even with the purple stain, she could still see the rainforest with Doctor

Judy Moody in the very middle. And none of the Band-Aids had come off.

"Never mind," said Judy.

"Never mind?" asked Dad.

"It's OK," she said. "At least it didn't get run over by a bus in a tornado."

"It's OK?" asked Stink. "You mean you're not going to put a rubber foot in my bed or anything?"

"No," said Judy. She grinned at her brother. "But that is a good idea."

"Look, honey. I know you worked for ever on this. We'll make it up to you somehow."

"I know what to do. Stink, let me have your black marker."

They all went out into the hall, and

Stink dug a marker out of his backpack. Judy set the collage on the floor and drew a black outline round the big purple triangle.

"Are you cuckoo?" asked Stink. "That's just going to make it stand out more."

"That's what I want," said Judy. "Then it'll look like it was supposed to be there all the time."

"I'm proud of you, Judy," said Dad.

"The way you took an accident like this and turned it into something good."

"What's it supposed to be?" Stink asked.

"Virginia," she said. "The state of Pocahontas and Thomas Jefferson. The place WHERE I LIVE."

Band-Aids and Ice Cream

When Judy got back to class, she put on her doctor coat, walked to the front of the room and held her Me collage high. She stood tall, as if her brother had not nearly ruined her masterpiece with Jungle Juice. She tried to look like a person who would grow up to be a doctor and make the world a better place. A person who could turn a bad mood right around.

Judy told about herself and her family, including the time Stink sold moon dust, which explained why her brother was a piece of dirt. She traced the outline of Virginia with her finger to show where she lived. She talked about Rocky, her best friend, and Frank, her new friend. She pointed to a paste jar lid taped to a corner and told the class that Frank ate paste for a dare once.

"Is that Jaws?" asked Brad. "The thing that eats bugs?"

"Yes," said Judy. "Even though I have a cat, Jaws is MY FAVOURITE PET. When I grow up and become a doctor, I want to move to the rainforest and search for medicines in rare plants that could cure ucky diseases."

Judy pointed out the pizza table from Mr Todd and other stuff she collected for HOBBIES. She told the class that she was a member of the TP Club, but that she couldn't tell them what TP stood for.

"This is a picture my parents took of Stink, standing outside the White House in his flag costume." And she explained why it was THE WORST THING THAT EVER HAPPENED to her. Everybody's favourite part of her collage was when she showed the doll hand, coming out of a magazine toilet. So Judy told them about how the worst thing ever turned

into THE FUNNIEST THING EVER.

"Any questions?" she asked the class.

"Who's the old lady?" asked Frank.

Judy explained about Elizabeth Black-well, First Woman Doctor, and then gave a demonstration of her doctor skills. She put Rocky's arm in a sling and wrapped bandages round Frank's knee. She pulled out her pretend blood, and used Hedda-Get-Betta to show how to apply Band-Aids.

"That's it. Me. Judy Moody."

"Great job, Judy," said Mr Todd. "Class, any comments?"

"I like how you painted Virginia in the middle of your collage to show where you live," said Jessica Finch, "instead of just using a picture of your house."

"Those Tattoo Band-Aids are the coolest," said Dylan. "I have a blister. Can I have one?"

"I have a hangnail!"

"I have a paper cut!"

"I have a mosquito bite!"

Before Judy knew it, everybody in the whole class was wearing Tattoo Band-Aids.

"Judy Moody, you're a mover and a shaker," said Mr Todd.

"I am?" asked Judy. "What's that mean?"

Mr Todd laughed. "Let's just say it means you have imagination."

What had almost become a bad-mood

Friday had turned into one very fine day. And it wasn't over yet.

When she walked out to get the bus that afternoon, Mum and Dad were waiting to take Judy and Stink for ice cream at Screamin' Mimi's.

"I'm getting that blue ice cream, Rainforest Mist. Like you guys always do!" Stink jumped up and down, holding his pocket with the toad.

"Did your teacher like Toady?" Judy asked.

"Yes, but she was almost in the Toad Pee Club," said Stink. Judy cracked up.

"Mum, Dad, can I ask Rocky and Frank to come too?"

"That's a great idea," Mum said.

Outside Screamin' Mimi's, Judy licked her Rainforest Mist scoop on top of Chocolate Mud, her favourite. She was in her best Judy Moody mood ever.

Stink took Toady out of his pocket and set him on the picnic table. Toady hopped towards a blue drip from Rocky's ice cream cone.

"Toady likes Rainforest Mist!" said Rocky.

"Hey, Frank," Judy asked, "when are you going to finish your Me collage?"

"Mr Todd said I could bring it on Monday."

"You're not done yet?" asked Rocky.

"I *still* don't have anything for CLUBS. The dictionary says a club is three or more people."

Judy looked at Rocky. Rocky looked at Stink. Stink looked at Judy. All three of them looked at Frank.

"If you pick up Toady right now, you can be in a club," said Judy.

"Really?" asked Frank.

"Really and truly," said Judy and Rocky at the same time.

Frank crinkled his nose. "I don't get it."

Rocky laughed. "You will."

Frank scooped up Toady with one hand.

"Use both hands," said Judy.

"Like this," said Rocky, cupping his hands.

"Just hold him a minute," said Stink.

"I still don't get it," said Frank.

"Oh, you'll *get* it," said Judy, Rocky and Stink.

A second later Frank felt something warm and wet in his hand. He crossed his eyes, and they all fell down laughing.

Judy Moody
Gets Famous!

For Kendra and Mary Lee
M. M.

For Mum and Dad
P. H. R.

Table of Contents

Judy

Who's Who

Roar!
Star of the show,
famous for her
many moods.

Dad

Judy's father.
Good at crossword
puzzles, quiz shows
and garage sales.

Mum

Judy's mother.
Former glee club
member. Knows her
vegetables.

Stink

Judy's scene-stealing
younger brother and star
of the Moody Hall of Fame.

Mouse

Judy's cat.
Amazing contestant
in the Fur & Fangs
Famous Pet Contest.

Rocky

Judy's best friend
since FOR EVER and
owner of a disappearing
Superman ring.

Mr Todd

Judy's teacher,
aka Mr Toad,
world's greatest
third grade teacher.

Frank

Judy's paste-eating friend
and one quarter of a
human centipede.

Jessica

Judy's classmate,
Jessica *Aardwolf* Finch,
aka know-it-all
Queen of the Spelling Bee.

How Do You Spell *Famous?*

Judy Moody marched into third grade on a plain old Thursday, in a plain old ordinary mood. That was *before* Judy got stung by the Queen Bee.

Judy sat down at her desk, in the front row next to Frank Pearl.

"Hey, did you see Jessica Finch?" asked Frank in a low voice.

"Yeah, so? I see her every day. She sits catty-cornered behind me."

"She's wearing a crown."

Judy turned to look at Jessica, then whispered to Frank, "Where'd she get that? Burger Barn?"

"I don't know," said Frank. "Ask her. She says it's bejewelled."

"Well, it looks be-dumb, if you ask me," said Judy, though secretly she admired the sparkling ruby-like gems.

"Hey, are those real rubies?" Judy asked Jessica.

"They're costume jewellery," Jessica said.

"Who are you dressing up as? The Queen of England?"

"No, I'm the Queen Bee," said Jessica. "I won the NV Spelling Bee on Saturday."

"The envy spelling bee?" Judy asked.

Judy didn't envy anybody who had to spell long words into a microphone with a million and one people staring bug-eyed at her. She knew those people were silently yelling *FLUB IT UP* because they wanted their own kid to win.

"Not *envy*. NV. As in Northern Virginia."

"Oh," said Judy. "Is that where you got the crown?"

"It's a tiara," said Jessica. "T-I-A-R-A. A tiara is a fancy crown like the Queen of England wears. Queen of the Bee has to know tons of definitions."

"What word did you win for?" Judy asked. "Frank wants to know," she added, in case Jessica thought *she* was interested.

"*Artichoke.* It's a fourth grade word."

Artichoke! Judy could barely spell *meat loaf*! Give me S-C-I-E-N-C-E any day, she thought. Was that the rule? *I* before *E*? Or was it *E* before *I*?

"I have spelling posters in my room at home," said Jessica. "With all the rules. I even have a glow-in-the dark one."

"That would give me spelling night-mares. I'll take my glow-in-the-dark skeleton poster any day. It shows all two hundred and six bones in the body!"

"Judy," said Mr Todd. "The back of your head is not nearly as interesting as the front. And so far I've seen more of it today than I'd like."

"Sorry," said Judy, facing front again.

Jessica tapped Judy and passed her a folded page from the newspaper. Right there, SMACK DAB in the MIDDLE of the newspaper for the whole world to see, was a picture of Jessica Finch. It even said LOCAL GIRL BECOMES QUEEN BEE in big fat headline letters.

"My dad says I got my fifteen minutes of fame," Jessica whispered to the back of Judy's head.

Judy did not turn around. She was green with NV. Jessica A. Finch, Queen of the Dictionary, Class 3T, was famous! Judy could not help thinking how stupendous it would feel to be able to spell better than *meat loaf* and be the Queen Bee and wear a tiara. To get her own picture in the paper!

But she, Judy Moody, felt about as famous as a pencil.

As soon as Judy got home from school, she decided to memorize the dictionary. But she got stuck on *aardwolf.* Three lousy words. Who ever heard of an aard*wolf* anyway? Silly old termite-eater. It had a pointy little head and beady little eyes and a pinched-up face that looked just like … Jessica A. Finch! Jessica *Aardwolf* Finch might be famous, but she was also a silly old termite-eater.

Since Jessica had become Queen Bee with the word *artichoke*, Judy decided to skip the dictionary and spell all the vegetables in the refrigerator instead.

"Do we have any artichokes?" Judy asked her mother, opening the door of the fridge.

"Since when did you start liking artichokes?" asked Mum.

"Don't worry, I'm not going to eat them or anything," said Judy. "It's for Spelling."

"Spelling?" Stink asked.

"Mr Todd does have some creative ways of teaching Spelling," said Mum.

"Never mind," said Judy, giving up when she saw asparagus. Vegetables were

too hard to spell. There had to be a food group that was easier.

At dinner Judy slurped up a noodle and asked, "How do you spell *spaghetti*?"

"N-O-O-D-L-E," said Stink.

"S-P-A-G-H-E-T-T-I," said Dad.

"Or P-A-S-T-A," said Mum.

"Never mind," said Judy. "Please pass the B-R-E-A-D."

"How was school today?" Mum asked.

"W-E-L-L," Judy said. "Jessica Finch won a T-I-A-R-A in a spelling bee and got her picture in the P-A-P-E-R. Even if she does look like an A-A-R-D-W-O-L-F, aardwolf."

"So that's what all this spelling is about," said Mum.

"You're W-E-I-R-D," Stink told his sister.

"*I* comes before *E*, Stink. Except after *C*. Everybody knows *that*." What a meat loaf.

"Actually," said Mum, "your brother's right."

"WHAT?" said Judy. "How can he be right? He broke the rule!"

"Lots of rules have exceptions," said Dad. "Times when you have to break the rule."

"No fair!" Judy slumped down in her chair. She was not going to become famous by spelling, that was for sure. The three strings of spaghetti left on her plate made the shape of a mean face. Judy made a mean face back.

Dad took a bite out of his garlic bread

and asked Judy, "You're not in one of your famous moods again, are you?"

The Moody Hall of Fame

The next day at breakfast Judy ate her cornflakes without even spelling them.

There had to be lots of ways people got famous besides spelling.

While she munched, Judy watched her little brother, Stink, hang stuff up on the refrigerator: his report card, the self-portrait that made him look like a monkey and a photo of himself in his flag costume, from the time he went to Washington, DC

without her. Above everything he had spelled MOODY HALL OF FAME with letter magnets.

"Hey!" she said. "Where's me?"

"*I* made it," said Stink.

"Why not leave Judy some room, honey," said Mum. "She can hang things there too."

Judy ran back up the stairs, two by two. She searched her desk for things to put in the Moody Hall of Fame. But all she could find were rumpled-up papers, acorn hats, a year-old candy heart that said HOT STUFF, and a drawer full of pink dust from all the times she had erased her spelling words and brushed them into her top drawer.

She rummaged through her closet next. All she had there were her collections: Band-Aids, fancy toothpicks, body parts (from dolls!), Bazooka Joe comics, pizza tables. Forget it. A person could not be in a hall of fame for toothpicks and Band-Aids.

Then Judy remembered her scrap box. Most kids, like Stink, had a scrapbook. What Judy had was a shoebox that smelled like old rubber. She stood on a chair and lifted the box down from the top shelf.

A lock of baby hair! A tooth she lost in first grade. Mum and Dad would never let her hang dead hair up on the fridge. And nobody wanted to see an old yellow tooth every time they opened the refrigerator. Judy came across a macaroni picture of herself in kindergarten, with a screaming O for a mouth. She put it back. Stink would just love the chance to call her a noodle head. And remind her that she had a big mouth.

Where were her report cards? There had to be some good ones. Certificates? Blue ribbons? She must have won something, sometime. But all she found were baby footprints, half-melted birthday candles and dopey drawings of people with four eyes that she'd scribbled in pre-school.

What about pictures of herself?

Pictures! Judy flipped through some old photos in an envelope. She had to find something as good as the picture of Stink the time he met the president. Here she

was with Santa Claus. But Santa looked like he was snoring. And there she was standing next to Abraham Lincoln (cardboard). No way could she be in the Moody Hall of Fame for having her picture taken with a cardboard president.

Then there was the one where she was face down on the neighbour's driveway, throwing a tantrum, because she did NOT want to get her picture taken.

It was no use. Judy could not think of a single thing famous enough for the Moody Hall of Fame.

Judy went back down to the kitchen. The letter magnets on the fridge should have said THE STINK HALL OF FAME.

"So? Where's your stuff?" Stink asked.

"Did you leave it upstairs or something?"

"Or something," said Judy. She hadn't even found the crummy old ribbon from the time she won the Viola Swamp Lookalike Contest in first grade.

"Mum?" Judy asked. "Did you ever get your picture in the paper?"

"Sure," said Mum. "Lots of times. For the high school glee club."

"What's *glee*?" asked Stink.

"*Glee* means being happy," Mum told him, "or cheerful."

"They put your picture in the paper just for being happy?" asked Judy.

"No." Mum laughed. "Glee club is a singing group."

Judy did not think anybody would take

her picture just for being happy. Or for singing songs about it.

"How about you, Dad?" asked Judy.

"They said my name on the radio once for having the right answer to a quiz-show question."

"What was the question?" asked Stink.

"How many presidents were born in Virginia?"

"How many?" asked Stink and Judy.

"Eight."

"Wow," said Judy.

"Aren't you going to ask me?" asked Stink.

"You never had your picture in the paper," said Judy.

"Yes, I did, didn't I, Mum?" Stink asked. "It's in my baby scrapbook."

"You've heard that story, Judy, about how we waited too long to leave for the hospital and your brother was born in the back of the Jeep."

"I was even on TV! On the news!"

"Oh, yeah," said Judy. "Thanks for reminding me."

It wasn't fair. Her own stinky brother got to be on the real live news. She, Judy Moody, was not even famous enough for the refrigerator.

Infamous

Rocky was already waiting for them at the manhole.

"Hey, Rock," said Stink, "did you ever get your picture in the paper?"

"Sure," said Rocky. "Bunches of times."

"You did?" asked Judy.

"No, not really," said Rocky. "But they did hang my picture up in the library one time."

"See?" Judy said to Stink. "Even my best friend is famous."

"Why'd they hang your picture up in the library?" asked Stink.

"My mum took me to the library to see this magician guy, you know? He did this trick where he took my Superman ring and made it disappear. Then he pulled it out of his sleeve along with a bunch of scarves. They took a picture of it and I'm the kid in the front row with my eyes bugging out. Not exactly famous."

"Still," said Judy.

When Judy got to school, Mr Todd said, "Let's go over our spelling words." Spelling, spelling, spelling. The whole wide world was hung up on spelling.

Judy leaned over and whispered to Frank. "Hey, Frank, ever had your picture in the paper?"

"It's no big deal," said Frank. "I was three years old."

Adam stood up and spelled the word "R-E-C-Y-C-L-E".

"What was it for?" whispered Judy.

Hailey stood up and spelled the word "I-C-I-C-L-E".

"I won the Grandpa Grape Colouring Contest in the newspaper. You had to colour this dancing grape cartoon guy. He used to be on grape juice. I couldn't even stay in the lines."

Randi stood up and spelled "M-O-T-O-R-C-Y-C-L-E".

Even Frank Pearl was famous. For scribbling on a dancing grape.

"Everybody I know is F-A-M-O-U-S," Judy grumped.

"Judy," said Mr Todd, "were you hoping to get a white card today?"

A white card! Three white cards in one

week meant you had to stay after school! She already had two. And it was only Wednesday.

"Why don't you spell the bonus word aloud for us?" Mr Todd said.

Bonus word? thought Judy. She hadn't been paying attention. She, Judy Moody, was in a pickle. Pickle? Was that the word? "Could I have the definition please?" she asked.

The whole class cracked up. "It's something you eat," said Rocky.

Judy stood up. "P-O-P-S-I-C-L-E. *Popsicle*," she announced confidently.

"Very good," said Mr Todd. "For *Popsicle*. Unfortunately that wasn't our bonus spelling word for today. Jessica? Would you

like to spell the word for the class?"

Jessica Finch stood up tall, holding her pointy head so she looked very queenly. "P-U-M-P-E-R-N-I-C-K-E-L. *Pumpernickel,*" said Jessica, faster than necessary.

Pumpernickel was one of those artichokey kind of words that only Pinch Face herself could spell. I bet she can't spell *aardwolf,* thought Judy.

"Judy," Mr Todd said, "if you study your spelling words and pay attention in class, you can avoid getting white cards and we'll both get along famously."

There it was again. *That word.*

It was almost time for Science, her best subject, so it would be easy for Judy to pay

197

attention. She'd sit up straight and raise her hand a bunch, like Jessica Finch.

She, Judy Moody, would *not* get another white card.

ø   ø   ø

Judy studied the squirming worm on her desk up close.

"As you all know," said Mr Todd, "we've been raising mealworms. Today I'm passing one out for each of you to examine. You can often find mealworms at home. Where do you think you would find them in your house?"

Judy raised her hand.

"They like to eat oatmeal and flour and stuff," she said when Mr Todd called on her.

"So maybe in your kitchen?"

"Right. Good," said Mr Todd. "They are actually the larvae of a type of beetle. The flour beetle. Mealworms are nocturnal," said Mr Todd. "Who can explain what that means?"

Judy's hand shot up again.

"Judy?"

"They sleep in the day and wake up at night," said Judy.

"Fine," said Mr Todd. "This kind of mealworm is called a *T. molitor*. Everyone take a minute and count how many segments you find on your mealworm. Then write it down in your notebook."

Judy counted thirteen segments, not

including the head. She wrote it in her notebook right away. While she waited for the next question, she let the mealworm climb up her finger. She let it climb up her pencil. Rare! The mealworm perched on her eraser.

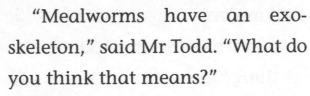

"Mealworms have an exoskeleton," said Mr Todd. "What do you think that means?"

Judy knew everything about bones and skeletons. Inside ones and out. She knew the answer again. Judy shot her hand straight up in the air. Judy forgot about the pencil in her hand. She forgot about the mealworm on the tip of her eraser.

Mr Todd called on Rocky.

Judy watched her mealworm fly through the air. She watched it land smack dab on Jessica Finch. She watched it crawl up the front of Jessica's shirt and right up onto the tip of Jessica's ponytail.

Judy forgot all about the white card. She waved her hand wildly at Jessica until Jessica looked up, then pointed frantically at Jessica's head.

"Aaagh!" Jessica screamed worse than a hyena and flicked her hair to shake off the mealworm. *T. molitor* sailed through the air, hit the chalkboard and fell to the floor. Class 3T went wild.

"Class!" said Mr Todd, clapping his hands. "Everybody quiet down. Jessica," he said.

"I'll not have anybody throwing mealworms in my classroom." He wrote her name on the board.

"But I didn't … it was … she did!"

"That's enough. See me after Science for a white card."

Jessica glared squinty-eyed at Judy. Her pointy ears looked pointier. Her pinched-up face looked even pinchier. Judy faced front.

Judy knew it was all her own fault. But she did not want to get a third white card.

Jessica Finch probably never got a white card before, thought Judy. She probably didn't even know before today what it felt like to get in trouble. All Jessica had was one puny little white card, and one puny little white card never hurt anybody.

For the rest of the morning, Judy felt more and more like a bug. No, a louse.

After lunch, her neck started to itch. Then her elbow. She scratched her left knee. Her toe itched inside her shoe.

By the end of the day, Judy went to talk to her teacher. "Mr Todd," she asked, scratching her ankle, "do you think not telling the truth can make a person itch?" *Scratch, scratch, scratch.*

"I think so," said Mr Todd. "Is there something you're itching to tell me?"

"Yes," said Judy. *Scratch, scratch.* "In Science today?" *Scratch.* "It was my mealworm." *Scratch.* "My fault." *Scratch, scratch.* "Not Jessica Finch's."

Judy told the whole truth.

"Thank you," said Mr Todd. "I appreciate your coming to me with the truth, Judy. I know that's not always easy."

"Does this mean I don't have to get a third white card?"

"I'm afraid not," said Mr Todd. "I still want you to learn to pay better attention."

Mr Todd erased Jessica's name on the board and wrote Judy's name in its place. Judy hung her head.

"Honestly, it's not so bad staying after school with me. We'll find something useful to do, OK? Like maybe clean out the fish tank."

"Mr Todd, is there a word for somebody

who gets famous for all the wrong rea-
sons?" asked Judy.

"Yes," said Mr Todd. "That would be ...
infamous."

Fame is the Pits

Judy peeled a banana.

"Can I have that?" asked Stink. Judy handed him the banana peel.

"Not *that*!" said Stink.

Judy took a monster bite, then handed Stink the banana. She picked up a cherry instead.

"What are you writing?" she asked her dad, popping the cherry into her mouth.

"Garage sale," said Dad. "I'm running an ad in the paper. It's time to get rid of all that old stuff out there."

"Old stuff?" asked Judy, perking up. Old stuff got people in the newspaper. Really really old stuff even got people on TV. "What old stuff?"

"Your old bike, Mum's books from college, Stink's baby clothes."

"Don't we have any old-old stuff?"

"There's Dad," said Stink.

"Thanks a lot," said Dad.

"No. I mean like Cleopatra's eyelash," said Judy. "Or a hammer used to build the Statue of Liberty. You know. Stuff old enough to be really worth something."

"Stuff you didn't know you had and you find out you're rich?" Stink grinned. "Like antiques from your great-great-great-grandmother? You go on TV and they tell you it's worth a bunch of money."

"I'm afraid nobody's going to get rich around here. Our old stuff is junk," said Dad.

"ROAR," said Judy. She pulled the stem off another cherry.

If only she had something unusual. Really rare. Like maybe a broken plate from another century, or an old letter from the American Revolution.

"So, what's happening in school these days?" Dad asked.

Judy sat up. Had Dad heard about the white cards? "What do you mean?"

"I mean, is anything interesting going on?"

"Can I stay after school on Friday?" asked Judy. "Mr Todd says I can help clean the fish tank."

"P-U," said Stink.

"We'll see if Mum can pick you up. How about you, Stink?"

Judy popped another cherry into her mouth.

"We learned this funny story about George Washington," said Stink. "It's about not telling a lie."

Judy chomped down on the cherry.

"See, he chopped down this cherry tree. And when his dad asked who did it, Washington said, 'I cannot tell a lie.' And he told on himself."

Judy almost choked. She spat out her cherry pit. It went zinging across the table at Stink.

"Hey," said Stink. "She spat at me."

"It was an accident," said Judy.

"Judy!" said Dad.

"OK. OK. I cannot tell a lie. I coughed a cherry pit at Stink."

"Pick up the cherry pit," said Dad.

Judy reached under Stink's chair and picked it up off the floor.

"No fair," said Judy. "Why should anyone

get famous for telling a lie? The whole story about the lie is a lie!"

"Most people don't realize it's not true," said Dad.

"It's still a good story," said Stink.

Judy turned the cherry pit over and over. It gave her a brilliant Judy-Moody-Gets-Famous idea. A two-hundred-fifty-year-old idea.

Judy took the cherry pit upstairs to her room. She got out her hairdryer and turned it on HIGH.

"What are you doing?" asked Stink, who had followed her upstairs.

"What does it look like?" said Judy. "I'm blow-drying my cherry pit."

"You're nuts," said Stink.

After he left, Judy got out the tiny hammer from her doctor kit, the one for testing reflexes. She tapped on the cherry pit to give it scars, so it would look old. Very, very old. Next she took a pin and carved the initials GW on the bottom. Then she took out her clear plastic bug-box, the one with the magnifying glass on top, and put the cherry pit inside for safekeeping, initials-side up.

"Rare!" said Judy. And that was the truth.

@   @   @

On the afternoon of the garage sale, Stink had his own table filled with tub toys, rusty Matchbox cars, Lincoln Logs, a rubber band ball, Shrinky Dinks that had already been shrunk, paper cooties, broken rhythm instruments and glow-in-the-dark bugs he made with his Creepy Crawlers machine.

Matchbox cars   Lincoln logs   glow-in-the-dark bugs

"Stink, nobody is going to buy that stuff," Judy told him.

"Yeah, right," said Stink. "And they're going to buy air?" he said, pointing to Judy's empty table.

"You'll see," said Judy. "I have something better than junk." She covered her table with a midnight blue tablecloth that looked like velvet. She put up a sign:

Genuine Cherry Pit!
from George Washington's
Cherry Tree
dates back to 1743
You Saw It Here (first!)

Then she set her magnifying bug-box in the middle of the table. Inside was – *ta-da!* – the FAMOUS cherry pit.

Judy added one more line to her sign:

5¢ A LOOK

She could hardly sit still. She wondered how long it would take the newspaper people to come and take her picture with the two-hundred-fifty-year-old cherry pit.

Little kids put a nickel in the can and said, "Wow, is that REALLY from George Washington's cherry tree?"

"I cannot tell a lie," said Judy. "It is!"

"Where'd you get it?" they asked.

"It's been in the family for ever."

"For ever since last week," said Stink. Judy turned on him with her stinging caterpillar look.

"How do you know it's really George Washington's?" they asked.

"Just look," said Judy. She opened the lid and lifted out the cherry pit. "It says GW right here. See?"

"Let me see," said a girl named Hannah. She showed her little brother. "GW. It's just like M&Ms."

"M&Ms!" said the boy, and popped the pit into his mouth.

"Ricky, NO!" said his older sister. But it was too late.

"Spit!" said Judy.

"Spit it out, Ricky!" said Hannah.

Ricky gulped!

"Oh, no! Did he swallow it?" asked Judy. "Stick your finger in his mouth. Is it still in there?"

"It's gone," said Hannah. "Say you're sorry, Ricky."

"M&Ms. Yum," said Ricky.

"This is the pits," said Judy. "Now what am I going to do when the newspaper comes?"

"Duh. Make another one?" said Stink.

Judy groaned. Judy moaned. In one gulp that kid had swallowed her famous two-hundred-fifty-year-old George Washington cherry pit. In one gulp Ricky the neighbour kid had swallowed Judy Moody's ticket to fame.

The only picture of *that* cherry pit would be an X-ray.

Famous Pet Contest

Stink counted his garage sale money at the kitchen table. *Clink. Clink. CLINK.*

"Stink, you're counting that money out loud on purpose," said Judy.

"I can't help it!" said Stink. "Mum, tell her. Money makes noise. When you have so much of it." He grinned.

Judy crumpled up the newspaper that had their garage sale ad in it. She stuffed it angrily into the trash.

"Recycle, please," said Mum.

"Whoa," said Stink. "The recycle queen put paper in the trash?"

"Can I use it to line Mouse's litter box?" asked Judy.

"Good idea," said Mum.

Judy uncrumpled the paper and spread it on the floor to flatten it.

EARLY BIRD SPECIAL!

GARAGE DOOR SALE!

FAMOUS PET CONTEST!

KISS BAD BREATH GOODBYE!

Wait! Did that say *famous*? Judy went back and read it again:

FAMOUS PET CONTEST

Bring your pet to
FUR & FANGS
this Saturday!

Enter your pet in our
famous pet-trick contest!

Have fun! Win prizes!

Winners will receive a
blue ribbon and a gift certificate,
and get their picture
published in the
NORTHERN VIRGINIA STAR!

Judy could not believe her eyes. "Where's Mouse?" she asked.

"Upstairs," said Mum.

"Here, Mousey, Mousey," Judy called.
Mouse came down the stairs and strolled
into the kitchen, looking for some lunch.

Judy scooped up her cat and kissed her

on the nose. "*Mww, mww, mwww.* You, the best, most wonderful cat in the whole wide world with tuna fish on top, are going to make *me* famous!"

Visions of blue ribbons and certificates with fancy writing danced in her head. "*And* I get my picture in the paper. Hey," she said to her family, "does anybody feel like a piece of toast?"

             ☺   ☺   ☺

When Judy hurried into Fur & Fangs with Mouse and Stink that Saturday, it was packed.

Clutching a piece of bread, she said, "Everyone in the entire state of Virginia must own a pet that can do a trick. Hey, there's Frank!"

"And there's Rocky," said Stink.

"You guys! Frank! Rocky! Over here!" Judy called.

Frank's dog, Sparky, sniffed a purple dog bone. Sparky sniffed Judy's ankle. Sparky sniffed a ferret.

"What trick does Sparky do?" Stink asked Frank.

"He jumps through a Hula-Hoop, don't you, boy?" said Frank.

"I brought Houdini," Rocky said, showing them his iguana. "If you scare him, like with a loud noise or something, he can make the end of his tail drop right off."

"Rare," said Judy.

She looked around at all the other pets. There were a rabbit and a turtle, a white rat named Elvis and a striped salamander. Judy saw a hamster racing on a wheel, a snake so still it looked fake and a shell that was supposed to be a hermit crab. Someone had even brought a stuffed monkey.

"Time for the contest!" yelled the pet store lady over all the squeaking and squawking, growling and yowling.

All the people with pets formed a circle. First was a dancing cricket. Then a turtle that rolled over and a rabbit that drank from a straw.

Polly the parrot sang the first five notes of "The Star-Spangled Banner". Judy caught herself clapping.

When it was Frank's turn, Sparky jumped through the Hula-Hoop three times and everybody clapped. Then Rocky could not get Houdini's tail to drop off. "Dogs make him nervous," Rocky explained.

Three pet tricks later, Polly was still singing.

Emily from school had a ferret named Suzy that brushed its own teeth. Stink liked it the best.

"But all it did was eat the toothpaste," said Judy.

When it was Judy's turn, she set up a toaster on the floor, dropped a piece of bread into the slot, then took Mouse out of her cat carrier.

"This is Mouse," Judy told the audience. "She's going to make toast." The audience clapped. Judy stood Mouse on the table.

"Don't be nervous," she whispered.

Mouse sat down and began licking her paw.

"Look at the toaster, Mouse," whispered Judy. "The toaster!" Judy pushed it towards Mouse.

Mouse swatted the toaster. Mouse swiped at the toaster. Mouse pushed the toaster away with her paw. Everybody cracked up. Judy held out a Tasty Tuna Treat. Mouse stood up. Mouse saw herself in the toaster!

Judy held her breath.

Mouse swiped at the toaster one more time. This time she pressed down the button with her paw. The slice of bread disappeared! The red coils heated up.

The crowd got quiet. A minute later,

the toast popped up.

"Ta-da!" called Judy.

"Hooray!" Everybody clapped and cheered.

"Mouse, I'll be famous at last!" Judy squeezed her.

"And now, last but not least," said the pet store lady, "a chicken that plays the piano."

Up stepped David, a boy with a chicken on a leash.

"This is Mozart," said the boy. Mozart pecked out three notes on the toy piano with his beak. "'Three Blind Mice'!" someone yelled. The crowd went wild.

Judy felt a familiar twinge, the tug of a bad mood. She, Judy Moody, would never

be as famous as a piano-playing chicken.

For the grand finale, everyone paraded their pets, marching in a circle.

"What a great contest this year," said the pet store lady. "I'd like to thank all of you for coming. Now, for the prizes," she said. "If I call your pet's name, please step into the centre of the circle."

A man stepped up to the circle with a big camera.

"The newspaper! They're here," Judy announced.

"In third place, Suzy Chang, the tooth-brushing ferret."

Please-please-please, Judy wished silently.

"Second place is Mouse Moody, the cat who makes toast!"

"That's you!" said Frank and Rocky, pushing Judy into the circle.

"Mouse, we won!" cried Judy. "Second place!" At last her time had come. At last her chance to be famous.

"And first prize goes to Mozart Puckett, the piano-playing chicken! Let's hear it for all the famous pets!"

The crowd went wild. Each pet got a blue ribbon to wear and a gift certificate to Fur & Fangs. The winners lined up to have a picture taken! Judy was on the end, holding Mouse, but Mouse squirmed and leaped out of Judy's arms. Flash! Judy blinked. The newspaper man snapped a picture faster than lightning.

"Thank you, everybody! That's it!" yelled the pet store lady.

"That's it?" asked Judy.

Judy's fifteen minutes of fame lasted only fifteen seconds. Fifteen seconds of fame, and she, Judy Moody, had blinked.

The following morning, Judy ran outside to fetch the paper. She whipped through the pages. Her heart beat faster.

"Here it is!" Judy cried. She could not believe her eyes. There were David Puckett and Emily Chang with mile-wide smiles. There were Mozart the chicken and Suzy the ferret.

"Let me see!" said Stink. "Hey, there's Mouse!"

"I'm not even in the picture!" yelled Judy.

"There you are!" said Stink, pointing to an elbow.

"I'm not famous!" Judy wailed. "I'm an elbow!"

"Let's see," said Dad. He read the caption. "Blah-blah, *winners of the Famous Pet Contest*, blah-blah. It says your name, right here. See? *Mouse and Judy ... Muddy.*"

"WHAT!" said Judy. "*Muddy?* Let me see."

"Judy Muddy! That's a good one," said Stink.

"Judy Muddy! No one will ever know it's me," said Judy.

"We'll know," said Dad.

Judy frowned. "I guess your name is Mud," Dad said, laughing.

"ROAR!" said Judy.

"At least it says Mouse won the contest," Mum said. She cut out the picture and hung it up on the fridge.

"Great," said Judy. "Even my cat's in the Moody Hall of Fame."

Mum kissed the top of Judy's head. "And you have one very famous elbow."

Broken Records

Judy studied her famous elbow in the mirror. She squished her elbow into a wrinkled happy face. She squinched her elbow into a mad face.

If Judy ever hoped to be more famous than an elbow, she needed some help. Judy called all members of the Toad Pee Club. "Meet at the clubhouse," she told everybody.

Rocky, Frank and Judy crowded into the blue tent in her backyard. Last was Stink, who carried Toady, their mascot, in one hand and walked while reading a book.

"Stink, you better watch out or you'll renew your membership."

"OH!" said Stink. He tossed Toady into the bucket before the toad famous for peeing in people's hands did it again.

"Now," said Judy, "how can we make me famous?"

"Let's think," Rocky said.

"Stink, you're not thinking," said Judy.

"Getting famous is boring," said Stink, leafing through his book.

"Stink, what book could be sooooooooooo interesting?"

Stink held up *The Guinness Book of Records*. Judy looked at Frank. Frank looked at Rocky. Rocky looked at Judy. "Brainstorm!" the three yelled at the same time. Then they cracked up.

"Stink, you are a genius. The secret to getting famous is right there in your hands."

Stink checked his hands.

"Don't you get it?" said Judy. "I could break a record and get in that book! Then I'd be super famous."

"Famous. Famous. Famous. YOU are a broken record," Stink told her.

"Hardee-har-har," said Judy.

"You know how you collect stuff, like

Band-Aids?" said Frank. "You could break a record for collecting something. Like the most pizza tables."

"Or scabs!" said Judy.

"Bluck," said Stink. "There's a guy in here who collects throw-up bags from aeroplanes. He has two thousand one hundred and twelve. One bag even has a connect-the-dots drawing of Benjamin Franklin on it."

"That's way better than scabs," said Judy.

"Hey, look," Rocky said, reading over Stink's shoulder. "World's longest word. Spell that and you could be the next Jessica Finch."

The word was *pneumonoultramicroscopic-silicovolcanoconiosis.*

"Whoa. Forty-five letters," said Frank, counting.

"Not even Queen Bee herself could spell that!" said Judy.

"It says here it's an ucky disease from volcanoes," Rocky said. "No lie."

"Wait! I got it. There's a guy in here with the longest neck," said Stink. "We could all pull on your head to stretch your neck out!"

"I want to be famous, not a giraffe," said Judy.

"With a giraffe neck you would be famous," Stink told her.

"Let me see that book." Judy grabbed the book of records and flipped through the pages. Longest gum wrapper chain? It took thirty-one years to make! Longest fingernail? No way; the guy hasn't cut his thumbnail since 1952. Best spitter? Judy could spit.

Then she saw it. Right there on page 399.

The human centipede!

"OK. Listen up. We're going to be a giant creepy-crawly," said Judy. "Let's tie our shoelaces together, then walk like a caterpillar. The old record is ninety-eight feet and five inches. Rocky, remember last summer we measured with a string? It was one hundred feet to your house and back. So all we have to do is walk from here to Rocky's and back to break the record."

They sat in a line, one behind the other,

like desks in a row. First Judy, then Frank, Rocky and Stink.

"Hey, I'm always last!" said Stink.

"You're the rear end," said Judy. "Tie one shoelace to the person in front, and one to the person in back," she called.

"How are we ever going to stand up?" asked Stink.

"On the count of three," Judy began. "One, two…" Judy took the first step. Frank's foot shot up and out from under him. Like bowling pins, Frank toppled sideways, Rocky fell over on his ear and Stink crashed on his elbows.

Frank snorted first. Rocky cracked up so bad he sprayed everybody.

"Hic-CUP!" said Stink.

When they were finally standing, without anybody falling or snorting or hiccuping, they each tried to take a step. One … two … three.

"The human centipede!" called Judy. She pictured the human centipede in her imagination – growing longer and longer, all wiggly and squiggly with tons of legs, and she, Judy Moody, at the head with biting fangs and poison claws!

"*Hssss!*" said Judy.

"No hopping, Rocky," called Frank.

"My lace is all twisted," said Rocky.

"Hold up!" yelled Stink from the end of the line.

That's when it happened.

Judy stopped, but the rest of the centipede kept going! They all began to fall. *Crunch!* Judy stepped on Frank's hand. Frank's other arm socked Rocky in the stomach. Stink's foot landed in Rocky's hair.

Three steps, and they had crumbled into a human pretzel.

"Hey! Watch it!" Stink yelled.

"I'm all twisted," Rocky said.

"OWWWWWWWWWWWWW!" Frank screamed. Frank was holding up his right arm with his left hand.

Frank Pearl's right pinky finger looked all floppy. It looked all floopy. Frank Pearl's pinky was twice as fat as normal and dangled down the wrong way.

"OOOH! What happened?" asked Judy.

"It hurts ... bad," said Frank, tears streaming down his face. "Real bad."

"Stink, run and get Mum. Fast!"

What if Judy had broken a finger, not a record? If Frank's pinky was broken, it was all Judy's fault.

Judy no longer felt like a human centipede. She, Judy Moody, felt more like a human *worm*.

Broken Parts

"So which one of you's the patient?" asked a tall man with a red beard in a long white coat.

Frank held up his little blue sausage of a finger.

"Ouch!" said the man. "How'd this happen?"

Frank looked over at Judy. Judy stared a hole in the carpet.

"We were playing," Frank answered.

"We were making a human centipede so my sister could be famous!" said Stink. "And she stepped on Frank!"

Judy sent Stink her best troll-eyes stare, complete with stinging caterpillar eyebrows. The man laughed. "OK. Well. I'm Ron, the emergency-room nurse. I'll take you back, and the doctor's gonna fix you right up, Frank. Is your mum or dad here?"

"My mum went to call Frank's mum," said Judy.

"OK. Tell you what. The Children's Wing is right through those red doors. Why don't you two wait in the playroom there. It'll be more fun. I'll tell your mum you're there, when she comes back."

Too bad Rocky went home. Now she

was stuck with Stink. They pushed through the red doors and into a long hallway. At the end of the hall was a room marked THE MAGIC PLAYROOM. Judy and Stink went in.

The walls were papered with teddy bears in hospital gowns, holding balloons. Each bear had crutches or bandages or sat in a wheelchair. There was a couch, a table with crayons and paper for colouring, a plastic castle and a bookshelf with books about going to the hospital. There was even a miniature operating table on wheels. The only kid in the playroom was a girl in a wheelchair.

"How come you're in a wheelchair?" Stink asked her.

"Stink, you shouldn't ask stuff like that."

"It's OK," said the girl. "I got a new heart. They can't let me walk around yet. They have to keep me at the hospital for a long, long time to make sure it works."

"A whole new heart! Wow!" said Stink. "What's wrong with your old one?"

"Stink!" said Judy, even though she wanted to know too.

"It broke, I guess," said the girl.

"Were you scared?" Judy asked.

The girl nodded. "Guess what. My scar goes from my neck all the way down to my belly button."

"What's your name?" asked Stink.

"Laura," said the girl.

"That's one brave heart you got there, Laura," said Judy.

"Daddy says I'm a brave girl," Laura said. "I'm getting a hamster when I go home. Do you have a hamster?"

"No," said Judy. "I have a cat named Mouse."

"There's nothing to do here," said Laura, looking around.

"They have doctor stuff," said Judy.

"Look! A real sling and stuff!" said Stink, kneeling next to a big cardboard box. He pulled out Ace bandages, boxes of gauze and tongue depressors. Even a stethoscope and a pair of crutches.

"Stink, can I put your arm in a sling?" Judy asked.

"No way," said Stink.

"How about you, Laura? I know how. For real."

"I'm sick of doctor stuff," Laura said.

"What about dolls?" Stink asked. "There's a bunch of dolls in this box."

"They all have broken arms and legs, or no heads," Laura said. "And some of them have cancer."

"What do you mean?" Judy asked.

"They're bald, like Sarah in my room."

"That's not fair," Judy said. "They should at least have dolls to play with that aren't sick."

The nurse came back just then. "Time to go back to your room," she told Laura. "Did you kids meet our brave girl?"

"Yes!" said Judy and Stink.

"I hope your new heart works great!" said Judy, as Laura left with the nurse.

"Bye!" called Stink.

Judy looked through the doll box. Laura was right. All the dolls were dirty or broken or hairless or headless.

Mrs Moody poked her head in the doorway. "Hello!"

"Mum!" said Stink.

"Is Frank OK?" Judy asked.

"His finger's broken," said Mrs Moody, "but his mum is with him now. He's getting a splint."

"Rare! A real splint!" said Judy.

"He won't be playing any basketball for a while, but he's going to be just fine. So. Ready to go?"

Stink and Judy followed Mrs Moody out of the playroom. Halfway down the hall Judy stopped, holding Stink back by his shirt.

"Stink," she said so her mum couldn't hear. "Give me your backpack."

"What?"

"Your backpack. I need it."

Stink made a face and handed over the pack.

"Catch up with Mum and tell her I forgot something. I'll be right back."

Judy dashed back into the playroom and over to the box of broken dolls. Looking around to make sure no one was coming, she stuffed the dolls into the backpack. Judy zipped it shut, flung it over her shoulder like a lumpy Santa Claus sack and headed back down the hall.

When Mum stopped to ask a question at the desk, Stink said, "Hey! What's in there?"

"Nothing."

"Nothing does not make a big fat lump.

Did you take that doctor stuff? You took stuff! You stole! I'm telling!"

"Shh! You can't tell anybody, Stink, or we'll get in trouble for stealing."

"We? You mean *you'll* get in trouble," said Stink. "Are you crazy? Do you want to be famous for being the only third grader who ever went to jail?"

"Swear you won't tell, Stink."

"What will you give me?"

"I'll let you look at real spit under my microscope."

"OK. I swear."

"You swore!" said Judy. "I'm telling."

Body Parts

As soon as Judy got home, she unloaded the backpack and spread the dolls out on her bottom bunk. She, Doctor Judy Moody, was in an operating mood. On her bed was a doll that didn't talk or cry any more, and one with no arms. There was a headless doll, and one that was bald.

First Judy gave each of the dolls a bath.

"I know just what I need," said Judy.

"Body parts!" She dug out her collection: long arms, skinny arms, brown legs, pink legs, middles with belly buttons, one bare foot, a thing that looked like a neck and all sorts of heads – small heads, fat heads, Barbie heads, bald heads! Judy emptied a whole bag of body parts onto her bed. "Rare!"

Judy glued a red wig with yarn braids onto the doll with no hair and gave another one arms that bent. Judy bent the arm back and forth, back and forth, to test it out. "Boo!" said the doll each time Judy lifted her arm.

"You don't scare me!" Judy told the doll.

"And for you," she said to the headless

doll. "A new head!" From all the heads on her bed, Judy chose one with brown hair and green eyes.

"There you go," said Judy, popping on the new head. But when she turned the doll upside down to put some shoes on her, the doll's head flew off and bounced across the floor!

"Whoa!" said Judy, running after the head. "That won't work. Let's try this one. How would you like eyes that can close and open?" Judy twisted the new head onto the doll's neck and waved her up, down, up, down through the air a few times to watch the eyes open and close.

"Voilà!" said Judy. She kissed the doll right on the nose.

Next she dressed each doll in a blue and white hospital gown she made from an old sheet, and gave each of them a paper bracelet printed with a name: Colby, Molly, Suzanna, Laura.

"Knock, knock," called Stink, pounding on her door.

"Go away," said Judy.

"Knock, knock!" said Stink.

"Who's there?" said Judy.

"I, Stink," said Stink.

"I Stink who?"

"I stink you should let me in your room," said Stink, letting himself in anyway. He peeked behind the blanket hanging over the bottom bunk.

"Aaagh!" he yelled, jumping back in shock. "Those dolls! The hospital – you stole! Those are … those aren't … if Mum and Dad find out…"

"Stink, you *promised* you wouldn't tell."

"Yeah, but…"

Judy was making a tiny cast out of oogey

wet newspaper. "Look, if you keep quiet, I'll let you help me."

"It's a deal!" said Stink.

Stink and Judy finished putting the cast on one of the doll's legs. When it dried, they painted it white and signed it with lots of made-up names. After that they made a sling for another doll, with a scrap of cloth. On a different doll Doctor Judy put tattoo Band-Aids from her Band-Aid collection all over its legs, arms and stomach.

"Double cool!" said Stink.

Last but not least was a rag doll made of cloth. Judy took a pink marker and drew a scar from the doll's neck down to her belly button. Then she drew a red heart, broken in two. With black thread she stitched the broken heart back together, hiding it under the doll's hospital gown.

"Just like that girl Laura!" Stink said.

When she was finished, Judy propped up all the dolls in a row on her bottom bunk and stood back to admire her work. She set her own doll, Hedda-Get-Betta, next to them.

"Wow, you made them look really good!" said Stink.

A little later Judy packed all the dolls into a box and secretly mailed them back to the hospital. Without a return address, no one would ever know that she was the one who had stolen the dolls.

It's like a real doll hospital, thought Judy. She, Judy Moody, was on her way to being just like First Woman Doctor, Elizabeth Blackwell.

Judy Moody and Jessica Flinch

On Monday morning Mr Todd asked, "Where's Frank today?"

"Absent," said Judy.

"Oh, that's right. I heard that he broke his finger. Does anybody know how it happened?"

"It's a loooooooooooooooooooong story," said Judy.

"As long as a centipede!" said Rocky.

"I heard Judy Moody stepped on him!"

said Adam. "CRACK!" He bent his finger back like it was breaking.

"OK, OK. We'll ask Frank all about it when he gets back."

"He'll be back tomorrow," Judy said.

Judy looked at the empty desk next to her. Without Frank, there was no one to snort at her jokes. Without Frank, she spelled *barnacle* with an *i*. Without Frank, she had nobody to tease about eating paste.

To make matters worse, all morning Jessica Finch kept inching her desk a little closer, a little closer to Judy.

"Is that the elbow that was in the paper?" Jessica asked.

Judy drew a mad face on her famous elbow and pointed it at Jessica.

"Hey, Judy? Want to come over to my house after school?" asked Jessica. "I could show you my glow-in-the-dark spelling posters."

"Can't," said Judy.

"Why not?"

"I have to feed Jaws, my Venus flytrap."

"How about tomorrow?"

"I feed it every day," said Judy.

"How about after you feed Jaws?" asked Jessica.

"Homework," said Judy.

The truth: by Friday Judy was almost bored enough to go to Jessica's. Rocky had to stay at his grandma's after school for a week because his mum was working late, and Frank could hardly do anything with a broken finger.

Too bad she had finished operating on all the hospital dolls so quickly. Making a cast was the best!

If only she could try making a bigger cast, on a human patient. But who? Stink would not let her near him with wet oogey newspaper.

Judy looked back at Jessica Finch. Maybe she did not look like a Pinch Face. Maybe she did not look like an aardwolf. Maybe she looked like … a doctor's dream. The perfect patient!

"Hey, Jessica," Judy asked, "how would you like to get your arm in a cast?"

"It's not broken," Jessica said.

"Who cares?" said Judy. "It's just for fun."

"Sure, I guess. Does this mean you'll come over? I can show you my spelling posters."

"How does today after school sound?" asked Judy.

❧   ❧   ❧

When Judy got to Jessica Finch's house, the two girls went up to Jessica's room. Judy looked around. All she could see were pigs. Pink pigs. Stuffed pigs. Piggy banks. A fuzzy piggy-face rug. Even Jessica's bed looked like a pig wearing a pink skirt.

"You like pigs!" said Judy.

"What was your first clue?" Jessica laughed in her hyena way.

Judy touched the spelling bee prize ribbons Jessica had hanging on the wall. Jessica showed Judy her scrapbook, with all the times her name had been in the paper.

"Wow," said Judy. "Did they ever spell your name wrong?"

"Once. Jessica Flinch!"

"Judy Muddy!" said Judy.

"Look! Here are all the spelling posters I made." Jessica pointed to the wall next to her bed.

"Hey, they're green. How come they're not pink too?"

"Because they glow in the dark. Wait." Jessica pulled down the shades and turned off the light.

The room lit up with glow-in-the-dark words. All the spelling words from Mr Todd!

BICYCLE
ICICLE
BREADSICLE
POPSICLE
RECYCLE
MOTORCYCLE

"What's a breadsicle?" Judy asked. "Is that like pumpernickel?"

"Hey, you're good," said Jessica. "See, I make up fake words and play a game to see if I can fool myself. Want to play? Or we could play the pig game. Instead of dice you get to roll little plastic pigs."

"What about making a cast?" said Judy.

"You're not going to break my finger or anything, like you did to Frank, are you?"

"No! Besides, it was an accident," Judy said.

"OK. So. What do we need?" asked Jessica.

"Newspaper. Water. Glue."

"This comes off, right?" said Jessica.

"Right," said Judy. There must be some way to get it off, she thought. "We have to let it dry first. Then we paint it."

"Can we paint it pink?" asked Jessica.

"Sure," Judy said. *Rare. A pink cast.*

"I'll go get some old newspapers," said Jessica.

When she came back, she said, "All I could find was today's, so let's hope my parents have already read it!"

Judy and Jessica tore the paper into strips. Judy could not wait to see the pink cast. This was her biggest operation yet!

Judy dipped paper strips into the sticky mixture and carefully placed them one by one on Jessica's arm.

"Ooh. It feels icky," said Jessica. "Are you sure this is going to work?"

Jessica was as bad as Stink. "Here," said Judy, handing Jessica more newspaper. "Tear up some more strips. I'm running out."

Jessica handed Judy a strip. At the top was the word PHANTOM. Jessica handed Judy another strip. STRIKES. A third. HOSPITAL.

"Stop!" said Judy. "Where's the rest of this story?" She peered at Jessica's arm. "Page B six. Where's page B six, huh?"

"Oh. I think I already ripped it up."

Judy tried to read Jessica's wet, oogey arm, but all she could make out were the

words *doll thief*. "What did it say?" she asked in a panic.

"Phantom strikes county hospital, or something."

"Or something, what?"

"I don't know. What's the big deal?"

Judy stood up suddenly, scattering paper strips everywhere. "I gotta go!"

"You what? Wait! My arm! You can't just... What about my pink cast?" But Judy was already out the door.

She, Judy Moody, Doll Thief, would be famous all right. For going to jail. Just like Stink said.

Judy Moody, Superhero

"Home already?" asked Mum. "How was Jessica's? Fun?"

"I ... did you ... where's ... the ... paper?" Judy asked, out of breath.

"Today's paper? Right here," said Dad, pushing it across the table towards Judy.

Judy flipped through the paper madly. But when she got to section B, all she saw was a giant hole.

"Who cut up the paper? Stink?" she said, shooting him her best stinging caterpillar eyebrow look.

"Oh, I did," said Dad. "Here, I tacked it up right here on the fridge."

He read out loud:

PHANTOM DOLL DOCTOR STRIKES
COUNTY HOSPITAL

On Saturday, October 17, Grace Porter, a member
of the nursing staff at County General, noticed that
several of the dolls that had been donated to the
hospital for its Magic Playroom were missing.

"Funny coincidence," said Mum. "That was the same day we took Frank to the hospital!"

"Ha. Funny," said Judy, trying to smile. Mum would not find it so funny when she learned that her only daughter was an all-out, true-blue, *I*-before-*E* thief.

Dad continued reading:

The missing dolls created quite a stir. Young patients
who use the Magic Playroom in the Children's Wing
spent days speculating as to the identity of the doll
thief.

"Isn't that where I found you two?" asked Mum. "The Magic Playroom?" Judy's mother sounded just like a detective. *Jail time.*

> Curiously, a mysterious package was received a few days later, with all the dolls magically cleaned, scrubbed, fixed or mended. Each one was tagged, dressed in a hospital gown and had been properly "doctored" with fancy Band-Aids, slings and casts.

Dad paused and said, "Hmm. Band-Aids." *Uh-oh,* thought Judy. *Evidence.*

> A special doll with a once-broken heart was given to patient Laura Chumsky, who recently underwent the hospital's twenty-ninth heart transplant. On behalf of Laura Chumsky and all the young patients, the hospital staff would like to thank the anonymous donor, the Phantom Doll Doctor, for this kind contribution.

"It sounds like one of the superheroes in my comics!" Stink said.

"That's quite a story," said Dad, grinning.

"Let me see that," Judy said. She had to see it, had to read it, with her very own eyes. "Phantom Doll Doctor," she repeated, touching the words in the headline. "Rare!"

"What a thoughtful thing for someone to do," said Mum.

"Wish I'd thought of it," said Dad, tacking the article back up on the refrigerator with a pineapple magnet. There it was, front and centre in the Moody Hall of Fame.

"Too bad," said Stink.

"What's too bad?" said Judy.

"I kind of wanted to see the inside of a jail."

"Hardee-har-har," said Judy, nervously glancing at her parents. But they were both grinning proudly. That's when Judy's brain began working on a brand-new Judy Moody idea.

She'd make a sign. Maybe set up shop in the garage. Get other kids to give her their broken dolls or old stuffed animals. Or she'd find some at yard sales. She would doctor them up and donate them to more sick kids in the Children's Wing at the hospital. Some could have Ace bandages, or fancy scars, or tubes for breathing. Maybe even an IV!

And it could all be in secret. The hospital would never know the identity of the Phantom Doll Doctor. The way nobody knew Superman was really Clark Kent, a nice, quiet reporter from the *Daily Planet*.

Rare!

For the first time in a long time, the once Judy Muddy felt more famous than an elbow.

She, Judy Moody, Phantom Doll Doctor, now felt as famous as Queen Elizabeth, as famous as George Washington, as famous as Superman.

Famouser!

Wouldn't Elizabeth Blackwell, First Woman Doctor, be proud!

Have you read them all?

Judy and Stink are starring together!

In full colour!

Be sure to check out Stink's adventures!

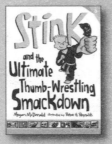

DOUBLE RARE!

Check out Judy Moody's interactive website at:

www.judymoody.com

Just some of its cool features:

- ◉ The Ultimate Judy Moody Fan Quiz
- ◉ All-new interactive games and a Mood Meter
- ◉ All you need to know about the best-ever Judy Moody Fan Club
- ◉ Totally awesome T.P. Club info!
- ◉ Digital downloads

Pssst! Go to www.stinkmoody.com to find out more about me, Stink!

10 Things You May Not Know About Megan McDonald

10. Megan shares a birthday – February 28 – with a famous princess, a race-car driver, a Rolling Stone, and a racehorse named Smarty Jones.

9. As a children's librarian, Megan told stories in sign language. That's where she learned the expression "same-same."

8. One summer, Megan and her four sisters tried to read ALL the kids' books on the bookmobile.

7. Megan still owns her original mood ring from the 1970s. She keeps it right next to her troll doll collection.

6. Who doesn't love insects? Megan has written five books about bugs, one of which is about eating them!

5. Megan's sister in Minnesota has a mailman named Jack Frost. No lie!

4. If ever there was a Crazy Socks Club, Megan could be a member. She has socks with sock monkeys, planets, gnomes, endangered animals, jellyfish, Popsicles, Girl Power, and comics. *Ka-pow!*

3. Megan is the proud owner of many Popsicle sticks with jokes on them, a sugar-packet collection featuring U.S. presidents, and what just might be the World's Biggest Jawbreaker.

2. Her favourite TV show is *Jeopardy!* Her secret wish is that someday Judy Moody will be a *Jeopardy!* clue.

1. Guess who used to live near the real Mt. Trashmore? Yours truly. For real and absolute positive!

10 Things You May Not Know About Peter H. Reynolds

10. He has a twin brother, Paul. Paul was born first, fourteen minutes before Peter decided to arrive.

9. Peter is part owner of a children's book and toy shop called the Blue Bunny in the Massachusetts town where he lives.

8. Peter has a son named Henry Rocket.

7. His mother is from England; his father is from Argentina.

6. He made his first animated film at age twelve.

5. He sometimes paints with tea instead of water – whatever's handy!

4. He keeps a sketch pad and pen on his nightstand. That way, if an idea hits him in the middle of the night, he can jot it down immediately.

3. His favourite candy is a tie between peanut-butter cups and chocolate-covered raisins (same as Megan McDonald!).

2. One of his favourite books growing up was *The Tall Book of Make-Believe* by Jane Werner, illustrated by Garth Williams.

1. And the number-one thing you may not know about Peter H. Reynolds is: he shares a birthday with James Madison, Stink's favourite president!

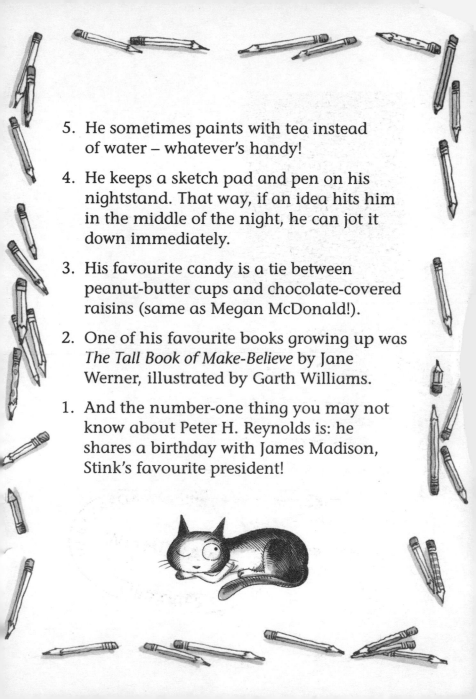